Devil on a Leash

by

J J Hughes

Bloomington, IN

authorHOUSE®

Milton Keynes, UK

AuthorHouse™
1663 Liberty Drive, Suite 200
Bloomington, IN 47403
www.authorhouse.com
Phone: 1-800-839-8640

AuthorHouse™ UK Ltd.
500 Avebury Boulevard
Central Milton Keynes, MK9 2BE
www.authorhouse.co.uk
Phone: 08001974150

First published by AuthorHouse 3/29/2007

ISBN: 978-1-4343-0570-1 (sc)

Printed in the United States of America
Bloomington, Indiana

This book is printed on acid-free paper.

This book is dedicated to

Sarah

"From whom do I expect forgiveness?" he wondered. If these poor unfortunate wretches, lying sprawled, twisted and frozen in the roadside ice had known all along that this was to be their fate, who of the them would have stood so bravely shoulder to shoulder, their call to arms their talisman? None, for in every man there is that cherishment of existence, in every man a desire to relish life and better their lot, but not for these unfortunates, their time was gone. For all time men were born equal, but there was no law that stated they should always remain that way, yet now there was no denying nature, these men were all equal in their fate.

With a wipe of the blood-soaked blade he calmly turned and walked back the way he had come, down a road that he always believed would lead to forgiveness. His actions were inhuman, his coldness shocked him, however this was not the first time this emptiness surrounded his every step, he had walked head bowed many times before and he would do so again he was sure, before his own fate reached its finale. He withdrew ashamedly from his work, moving in the shadows that had become his friend. Death still shocked him, the last moments, the last breath as the dying gasps slowed and gently ceased, he took no pleasure for there was no gain, his was a job and as much as it annoyed him, he was at times too good.

"Wake up Mr Blue, wake up" a voice bellowed from the overhang, a short squat man of Celtic extraction stood above him. Louis Blue shot to his feet, the sudden awakening startled him. For a man whose great gift to mankind was eternal sleep, it seemed ironic that sleep was the one token pleasure he sorely missed. Though no bad thing, as sleep led to dreams, dreams led to nightmares and nightmares led through to the morning. He recognised the voice and the solid shape of the man from where the command had emanated. Jonah Betts had a presence, a roughness honed on the back streets of some of Scotland's hardened districts. He said very little and acted upon orders. As a result it could be easily deduced that it would be unlikely he stood alone.

Lucifer Blue had no fixed abode. He was born as most of us are in a place we so easily forget. His past and his dreams had sparked in his memory so many times in union, that what was real and what was not simply didn't matter, he had no-one to question him and so therefore he could believe what he chose. He often pondered that with no family came no horizons, no duty, no blame. He was what he wished himself to be, but those thoughts belonged to what he called his 'sunny days.' In truth his life was an eternal winter, as wretched as those whose lives he would so often transport to dusk. As the light flickered away from their day, he would often be overcome by the understanding that what he was depriving them of he himself had never had. "Maybe" he would often muse, "Maybe one day my life will change."

"Mr Blue" whispered the softly spoken gentleman standing behind and a little to the left of his customary aide Jonah Betts. "How did it go Mr Blue? Were you successful Louis, were you? Oh I do hope you were, you don't mind if I call you Louis do you, it has been a while after all?" Lucifer had been a name Louis had christened himself at his own altar. For if he was to do these deeds, then he believed he should have a name that truly implied his labours. Through the years, because he could, he had expired his identity in a manner as cold as his usual labour. The early years, his last memory of sunshine had also taken their last dying gasps.

"You may call me that if you wish," Louis replied, loathing the attempt at kinship. This tall elegant man had no place in Louis' life. Well, in certain circumstances that would be true, but for the time being, here and now, the visitor had every reason to expect his agreement. After all they had met many times before, not always a surprise and in truth rarely a disappointment. Despite the hostility there was something about the visitor that Louis warmed to, perhaps it was that of all the people that walked the earth, the man standing imperiously above him looking down, was probably the closest Louis had to a friend, the mere fact he knew where to find him and would look into the piercing ice-crystal eyes of Louis in a manner quite endearing, allowed the natural scorn Louis carried for all to be gently replaced by a relaxed calmness. Whilst this would normally last only several minutes, it allowed Louis respite from his own hatred, he actually looked forward to these fleeting moments, but he would never let the visitor know that.

The gentleman's identity had been revealed many years earlier when Louis, on 'active service' had enjoyed a glass of ice-cold water with him following one of their clandestine meetings with which Louis had now come to terms. They were nothing more than formal de-briefings, never having to provide any form of evidence to testify his completion, over the years the results had spoken for themselves, the trust of the gentleman was one notable human quality that Louis was certain he had earned.

Louis himself had always impressed the man, not only for the exacting ease upon which his assignments were carried out, but also his appearance was as attractive as it was unique. Louis was tall, but yet not excessively so. His past had ensured he would always recognise the necessity of strength, both mentally and physically. He had broad shoulders and a confident walk, he held his head in an imperious fashion, but more for the fact he was always alert rather than for any grandiose consideration of his own importance. His hair was light brown and short and his eyes were an appealing blue. Their appeal had been remarked upon many times, but these eyes had been witness to countless horrific episodes, normally of his own doing. He would often reflect upon the fact that if your eyes were indeed the windows to your soul, that it was an almost comical irony that such eyes could reflect one such as his. Louis was handsome, yet he made no claims to his appearance, nor was he aware of the admiring glances he would often command. He saw no beauty in himself as it was only the inner perspective of existence that mattered to him, as his mind and soul were tortured, what else could he think.

Mr Abel Harrington, the otherwise ambiguous business card stated was the gentleman's identity and Geneva his address, but Louis was sure that if he ever had the time or inclination to make an impromptu visit, he would find himself looking down a road that was as empty as perhaps it was unrelated to the gentleman. With no telephone number and no other means of a trail, Louis was certain that whilst Abel Harrington knew all about him, in absolutely no circumstances would the gentleman reveal anything other than a name, a name that Louis in a very private thought prayed was real, everything else in this relationship was so bloody one-sided. He would give no more thought to the matter however, such pernicious thoughts were after all the domain of his prey. It was these little acclamations that provided Louis with his rationale and his separation from the tasks set. By removing any form of association with those lying mortally coiled beneath him, he knew his nightmares for the time being would be confined solely to his sleep.

Abel Harrington was of similar height to Louis, albeit a somewhat more slender individual. Likely to be in his late forties, he gave the appearance of one who had once been supremely fit. For any observer interested they would have probably suggested he was once a runner, perhaps at university and maybe also a keen cricketer. He hair was blond, pushed back and away from his forehead. He sported a small thin moustache. His features were very angular and his skin tanned, giving him the outward appearance of being very high brow. His dress sense did nothing to dispel this as on the many occasions they had met, he had always worn a cravat. A general assessment was that this particular gentleman would have not looked out of place thirty years earlier, but his appearance had an unusual validity to it that Louis in turn rather admired.

"A dreadful episode Louis." Abel Harrington remarked calmly peering into his teacup. If there was one pastime Louis felt he could associate with his visitor, it was that of drinking tea, no matter where or when the two men met, Abel Harrington would always drink tea. If pressed Louis was sure the reasoning provided would be that of a medicinal nature, but for now he was content imagining that the visitor was not a little eccentric and as was usually the way with such distinguished British gentleman, would never go very long without their nectar. The fact that outside the snow was still falling seemed completely irrelevant.

"Yet we must away old boy, the Soviets will have already expected us to hit them like this. They will have been prepared for such an eventuality, fortunately so are we my dear fellow, so come along now."

Louis grabbed his normal travel attire, a small bag concealing nothing but documents, forged and providing an identity which to Louis was as relevant as it was true. His disguises were never required for longer than several days at most. Just enough time to arrive, complete the 'termination' and then depart. Leaving no trace and no discernible evidence as to who was responsible. In time there would of course be the statutory finger pointing and the occasional tit for tat 'balancing items'. Yet Louis remained calm with the fact that these games were played at a level in which he took no interest, they were national, they involved governments, he was a pawn, a meagre foot soldier. However he was an extremely accomplished pawn and as long as this continued, then he was determined that this would always be the case.

Outside a rather luxurious Lada awaited. As many a true foot soldier can acclaim, a Russian winter can be quite damaging, not only to one's own morale and well-being, but also to that of entire nations. Louis for a moment pondered the fate of several so called invincible legions. The Nazis had made good in very similar vein to that of Napoleon's Grand Army, only for both to suffer ferociously from the frozen bullets that fell from the sky rather than any grape or automatic shot. Louis had time to feel a little professional pride, for it was on the edge of this little village late nineteen forty one, that the Nazis has attempted to swarm through the village of Aprelevka only to be driven back by thousands of Russian peasants. This village was the closest the Nazis ever managed to get to Moscow. Not only had Louis succeeded where Adolf Hitler had failed, he would turn the screw even further. The chain-draped tyres took the car with it's three passengers on a slow beat, winding the twenty five miles or so to Moscow. Deeper into 'enemy' territory the car took the men, the furthest reaches of the Third Reich had been surpassed.

There was an air of liberation in nineteen sixty eight and Louis sensed this through his travels more than most. Although his manifesto had one only directive, to obey his paymaster, the man who was sitting in the car with him, he felt no particular affinity to any ideology. This would probably after all lead to the eventual need to dispense with either a comrade or a brother, so Louis made the conscious decision to observe and try to keep these affairs of the soul at arms length.

There had been many demonstrations against the growing global capitalism and influence of western 'democracies.' In the United States earlier that year Martin Luther King had been assassinated, that had really pissed off the liberals and the enlightened thinkers. There were those who saw this event as a Soviet-influenced attempt to destabilize the heart of the Capitalist structure. Yet the following months had seen the unparalleled growth of the civil rights movement. There was no significant internal shift towards communism in the United States, though the oppressive enforcement of the Vietnam offensive did lead to many internal and external examinations as to the role of the most powerful nation on the planet. There were many demonstrations and in turn these were regarded as the formal expression of revulsion towards what was occurring on the global stage, yet they did little to disrupt the status quo. This test had been passed five years earlier with the Cuban missile crisis, so there was no reason to believe that things would change now.

Of course upheaval was not just a Western malaise. The Prague 'Spring' revolution brought reactionary atmosphere to the Eastern bloc too. The major states of the Warsaw Pact intervened to crush the tide of expression that had gained ground in a strikingly similar way to states in the West. There were the student riots in Paris, feminists were protesting against Miss World beauty contests and a picture was published of General Nguuyen Ngoc Loan executing a Vietcong prisoner. All this made Louis feel uncomfortable. People led to overt reactions or even killing when following some profound ideology was as alien to him as he felt certain his actions would be to society they ever be known. However this was his job and from that he found a moral code. To kill for a belief was just unjustified and corrupt, but why should he care, in all this mayhem, the one thing he could be certain of was that his particular skill was a significantly sought after precious commodity.

The car continued to weave unsteadily despite the grip of the chains covering the wheels. Turning into Traverskaya Street, Louis marvelled at the grey yet majestic nature of the 'curtain' buildings. Behind these, many of the old churches and buildings of the previous city had been hidden by the two-apartment-deep buildings built just prior to the war. The car skidded to a halt and out of a doorway approached a slight wispy man, dressed in standard Muscovite dress. He wore a large cap pulled almost suspiciously over his eyebrows to all but hide his face. "Good evening gentleman," the slight man offered.

Abel Harrington shook the man's hand vigorously, a degree of welcoming that Louis himself had never been afforded.

"Gentleman" Abel Harrington whispered. "May I introduce Willi van Noten. He will be our pilot."

Over the years, Louis had never ceased to be amazed by the number individuals who would surreptitiously emerge from the shadows to assist. There was never any logic to forming any kind of association with these people as Louis would only ever meet them once. He often wondered whether this was for security reasons or for the simple fact that he was a loner and life's hand would always make it this way.

The car moved off heading in the direction of Vnukovo airport with the four men inside, a new supply of false identification papers and a map of Berlin.

"Good," thought Louis, even by his standards the last twenty four hours had been above all extremely tiring. The idea of relative safety and comfort after these recent endeavours was particularly appealing.

As the small four seater Piper PA 28 taxied discreetly towards the runway, for the first time since being abruptly woken from his sleep did Louis feel a little alarmed. Around them seemed to be an array of Russian MIG combat fighterplanes. If there was any arousal of suspicion this particular battle would be very one sided. However, as the plane left the small runway on the far side of the airfield and disappeared into the low cloud, Louis looked back and was calmed by the stillness on the ground. This task had taken its toll in terms of his exhaustion, yet he could now relax back into his seat and look forward to supper in West Berlin.

Any exodus provides a certain degree of welcome, whether driven or of one's own undertaking. There is normally a reason to leave that leads to a departure. As the four men touched down in the West, a certain degree of calm filled the cabin.

As Louis stepped from the plane, Abel Harrington touched his shoulder and beckoned he follow him.

"Ahem! Listen Louis, you may have thought it a trifle odd, that I held your hand all the way home this time. You see my dear fellow, I have strict orders. The chaps at the ministry require a full debriefing, not with me you see, but with you, in London. Something has, how shall I put it, come up! My instructions are to ensure you arrive in London as soon as is convenient."

"That being when?" Louis immediately responded, resigned to the inevitable.

"Well let us have a nice cup of tea and see if our kind Mr Van Noten wouldn't mind a few more hours at her majesty's pleasure."

Abel Harrington had developed an obvious affinity with Louis, but by now any notion that Louis' day was over had very abruptly left his thoughts. He stared defiantly at his paymaster, gritting his teeth determinedly and leaving no one in any doubt that any warmth displayed over the preceding several hours in their cramped return to Berlin had been retracted in an instant.

"Bastard!" Louis muttered under his breath. Dejected by this treatment and exhausted from his exertions, Louis traipsed to the edge of the runway and looked towards the woods by the edge of the small exposed airfield. If he ran now, he could be lost forever. Yet he knew, if you run, it is not only the person that becomes lost but sometimes the soul. His existence was bleak enough. When you have very little in the first place, it seems a pointless exercise running in any direction. Besides, it had started snowing again, West Berlin was not his favourite place in winter and perhaps the tea may help after all.

It was now the early hours, thankfully the flight had been relatively calm. A cloudless night was a welcoming respite from the previous few days. It had been several months since Louis had last been in England. The quintessential weather that so identified the country in winter, notably rain, and a cold grey sky, was the undoubted norm at this time of year. Yet the clear night had heartened Louis. The thought of a sunny crisp morning, gently strolling along the embankment with only the odd civil servant passing by running dreadfully late. Eight forty five was mandatory after all in Ministry buildings, but for those who had missed their usual bus or tube, the lurch towards the revolving doors provided a spectacle that for any passer-by always brought a chuckle. For Louis it was merely a curious observation, in his eyes it was just merely bad planning.

The Ford Escort twin-cam wound its way through the Cambridgeshire countryside. The plane had landed at a small airport in Norfolk. Louis had become accustomed to not landing at the large international airports, the complexities of his existence had destined that wherever and whenever possible he should avoid public entry and exit from countries. He was very thorough in his job, destroying all evidence and removing any trace that he was ever there, but more sophisticated surveillance techniques required him and his sort to be ever more vigilant. International airports were the windows which each foreign agency could peer to witness the comings and goings of that particular state. Louis preferred to arrive through the back door unnoticed, anticipation could never be understated in his line of work.

He had still not spoken in any meaningful way to Abel Harrington since his comments early the night before in West Berlin. Immediately upon landing Jonah Betts and Van Noten departed the small airfield . Their involvement in this particular task had come to an end. But for Louis and Abel Harrington the Ministry driver in the Ford awaited them. "Two hours and we should be by the embankment" Louis thought to himself. He was surprisingly comfortable in such cramped conditions and with the heating turned up to counter the coldness outside, he leant his head gently against the side window.

A sudden jerk and Louis lunged forward in the rear seat, his automatic reaction was to grab the figure in front of him, the car screeched, rocking from side to side. The

Ministry driver struggled desperately to free himself of the lock wrapped around his throat.

"Louis!" barked Abel Harrington. "You've been asleep, now be a good chap and don't kill the driver. He's the only one who knows the way."

The car had come to a complete stop between a hedge and a rather dense looking oak tree, there was smoke slowly rising from the radiator. Fortunately the stunned driver, having nearly been choked to death whilst managing to avoid a head on collision was still able to reverse the damaged car back on to the road. Setting off again, for the next few miles the speed of the car rarely exceeded thirty miles per hour, however that mattered very little, for they had now appeared to have reached their destination.

Louis stepped out of the car and waited for Abel Harrington to arise in a rather ungainly manner. As a tall man the smaller Ministry cars were hardly conducive to a quick exit. Nevertheless he was now standing alongside Louis, a brisk turn of foot and both men strode towards the door. Five minutes prior to the journey's end, Louis had noticed a road sign pointing in a easterly direction, it read 'Dorking 5 miles'.

"Shame," Louis thought to himself, the opportunity for the walk along the Embankment, past Big Ben, through Victoria, a brief glance at Buckingham Palace, then back through Pall Mall to Whitehall would appear to have been lost.

For a moment it appeared completely senseless that he should never have heard of Dorking never mind where it lay in relation to London, admittedly for a well travelled practitioner he could often visit locations of various 'projects' without actually having any sense of where he was. It troubled him though, for a country he served so blindly that his geographical knowledge of the British Isles was so basic. Louis seldom slept for periods longer than two hours, however the aching he had felt in his arms and legs when awoken by the sudden jolt of the car, suggested he had been asleep for some time. This in turn left him in no doubt, Dorking could in fact be anywhere.

A rather large imposing door confronted them. From the outside the house had an extremely austere perspective. The grounds surrounding the property were extensive and appeared to represent the picture-postcard archetypal English countryside scene. The dwelling however seemed strangely at odds with its surroundings, this was a functional house and appearances are seldom misleading.

Abel Harrington pulled the Victorian door chain to announce their arrival. The building appeared to be at least two hundred years old. It amused Louis somewhat that although trivial, at some point there had been an attempt to modernise the house, although with regard to the exterior, on further examination the chorded chain seemed to have been the last addition.

After several moments footsteps could be heard in the distance. The house was very large and it was therefore conceivable that it could take the inhabitants some time to arrive at the door. It also occurred to Louis that it was as equally inconceivable that they were not expected.

The door opened and a young lady, no older than thirty stood in the entrance to the door. Her appearance immediately betrayed her. On his several visits to Whitehall, Louis had become extremely familiar with the Ministry secretariat. England and in particular London, had a 'swinging vibe'. Louis, whilst aware, had not felt comfortable with the fashion on the streets during his previous visits, the Ministry had provided him sanctuary, his ascetic dress code was unlikely to ever leave him out of place once inside the corridors of Whitehall.

The lady provided a customary handshake and moved to one side.

"Gentleman, I trust you had a comfortable journey? Please follow me to the drawing room. You are expected."

"Interesting" Louis whispered to Abel Harrington, who in turn seemed quite taken aback by what appeared to be an expression of interest in the young lady. Over the years, despite their time together being only fleeting, he had come to understand the nature of this highly unusual man. As a result this relative outburst, demonstrating an awareness of the opposite sex had been totally unexpected.

"Interesting" Louis reasserted, having had no reply. "Did you notice the car outside had a Dutch number plate?"

Abel Harrington shook his head and smiled. "No Louis, that passed me by." The truth however was very different, of course it hadn't. He was now all to aware why they were here.

The visitors were led into the drawing room. At the far end of the room sat two men, both in armchairs and both silhouetted against a roaring fire.

"Welcome men, please won't you join us? I must apologise, these rooms are awfully cold during the winter. Now what would you like to drink?

Louis turned to Abel Harrington and then in turn to the host and rather tentatively requested a whisky.

"Lagavulin acceptable young man? It's my favourite and so very very useful at this time of year."

Louis nodded and accepted the half full crystal glass. He was now able to see up close the man who had provided him with his whisky, a large individual with very little hair, dressed in standard country squire clothing. A very professional degree of tailoring was noted. He guessed Saville Row, not from the cut, as he was not well versed in such aspects of couture, but rather because all men who purchased their tailored suits tended to fit a certain stereotype. This was one such man. As the man returned to the fire, the use of a cane to assist him was evident, he slowed at the chair of the other man, who had for all this time kept his gaze fixed resolutely upon the fire.

"Mr Blue, let me first introduce myself," said the large man. "I am Colonel Benjamin Mallory and whilst I no longer tread the boardwalk so to speak, I play a very interesting role in the defence of this great and glorious country of ours. I am acutely aware of who you are and what you do Mr Blue. I am aware because it is I and my colleagues who provide you with your work, we know your every move, we are the shadow's shadow if you like."

For over ten years Louis had obeyed orders, receiving regular payments for his endeavours directly into his bank account in Geneva. At a postal point across the road from the bank, he received his directives, never giving too much thought to what kind of people could make so many enemies.

He understood why in the defence of the West, he was regularly requested to disappear deep into Eastern Europe, often operating as the vanguard of Nato forces. But Louis had found himself on many other occasions operational in states where there was no apparent political motive, but he was a professional, a cold blooded killer, he therefore simply and effectively completed his task and then disappeared again, or so he thought. He felt embarrassed he had never thought to question with whom the ultimate source of his control lay with. It was becoming all too apparent that soon he would find out.

"Louis," remarked the Colonel. "This country owes a great deal to men like you. While all these hippies and liberals are doing their damn best to destabilise the very noble fabric of our society, it is your actions and those of men and women like you that keep us strong."

Louis looked to the floor, he was not accustomed to praise, but the reference to others had left him slightly taken aback. He had never seen himself as belonging to any group, this was a feeling with which he was totally unacquainted. The fact that there were others just like him, men and women, immediately threw into doubt all rationale he had for what he was employed to do. Over the years he had come to view himself as a lone predator, he took pride in that he certainly knew how to eliminate people. There was no particular reference point, yet he had always believed there could be no-one who could plan and operate and ultimately succeed like he was able to. In the matter of a few seconds however, aspects of his existence came crashing in around him. He was now extremely thankful for the Lagavulin.

"However Louis," continued the Colonel, "We have asked you here for a particular reason." He motioned to his companion. "This gentleman is a great ally of our country, during the last war, his actions and deeds went a long way to helping defeat the Nazis. Gentlemen I would like to introduce you both to Mr Marco van Rijn."

The man stood up and shook both Louis' and Abel Harrington's hands.

"Gentlemen," he said in a very distinguished manner. The owner of the car outside had more than likely just been introduced. The accent was undoubtedly Dutch, but the refinement of not only the greeting but the appearance of the man gave Louis the distinct impression of wealth.

"It is indeed a great pleasure to meet you both. The Colonel is a very dear friend, he has told me that you Mr Blue will be able to help me, being that you are this country's best X class, you are indeed first among equals, *primus inter pares*."

"X class?" Louis responded. "Who or what is an X class?" He looked quizzically at first the Dutchman then the Colonel and finally Abel Harrington.

"That is simply the term we use for colleagues such as yourself Louis," replied Abel Harrington, "You're an individual, who whilst a highly effective servant of the state, remains hidden, it is in no-one's interest that your existence be known by anyone other than those that need to know. The X simply denotes a stealth mode operative."

"More like a bloody car," Louis thought to himself. The four of them sat down in front of the fire. Louis had the feeling that these two men were about to relay his next mission. He was not to be disappointed.

The Colonel took a substantial swig from his glass. Louis immediately realised that this was probably going to take a while. Nevertheless, the first fifteen minutes of the meeting had been far from dull, so he too saddled himself into the comfy leather armchair, waiting attentively for either man to begin. He kept his eyes resolutely fixed on the Colonel. The last thing he needed to do now was fall asleep again. There was absolutely nothing customary about the day so far, therefore Louis had no expectation that normality was about to be resumed.

"As I think I've already mentioned," the Colonel began. "Mr van Rijn has demonstrated over the last twenty five years, through both his actions and his deeds, what a friend to this country he has been. In the face of the Nazi menace, he demonstrated bravery, organising resistance throughout the entire Benelux region. His network and control of the local underground prevented the capture of many pilots in the latter years of the war. They were successful in ensuring that many of our crewmen were returned safely to these shores. In addition he and his comrades did everything in their power to undermine the Nazi lines of communication, instigating many acts of sabotage. It was undoubtedly a significant effort on his behalf and it is not in our nature to forget our friends."

Louis glanced across at Abel Harrington. He was convinced that this man had once been a gallant resistance fighter, but so had so many others all across Europe who had gone on to make the ultimate sacrifice during the period of occupation. Just as Louis was beginning to question in his own mind what Marco van Rijn had done to receive such acclamation, the Colonel continued.

"However, Marco's unswerving support for our country did not cease with the end of hostilities in nineteen forty five, far from it. In fact over the last twenty five years Marco has continued to supply us with information crucial to us in our much longer battle, that being the not insignificant threat of socialism and the Soviet Union."

For Louis, there was now something spectacularly exciting about the Dutchman. He had demonstrated that in a similar vein to Louis there was no particularly ideology involved. He just simply chose a side and got on with the task at hand. Risking one's life in the line of duty had always been an extremely invigorating experience for Louis, but to have done it for so long amazed him. Here standing in front of him was a kindred spirit, in years gone by he may even have been a mentor should their paths have ever crossed.

"Louis," the Colonel resumed. "Many of the targets provided to you over the years have come directly from information provided by Marco, many of our agents lives would have been lost if it hadn't been for the espionage and intelligence provided by him, so you see, when I say that Marco is not only a dear friend of mine but also of this country, my only error perhaps lies in my understatement."

"May I interrupt?" responded Louis directly upon the Colonel's sudden pause for breath. I am needless to say impressed and thankful to Mr van Rijn for his assistance over the years." Louis had no real affinity with the past. His perception was not based on any national identity. He had simply a gift for his craft, had been subsequently noticed and then employed to administer his art. However, he didn't feel at this stage a little bit of nationalistic chest-beating was out of place. "If I am not being impudent in any way and of course if I am, I request your forgiveness, but why, given all that has been said so far, have you brought me here today?"

"Because Louis, Marco has asked us to help him and I therefore believe we owe it to him." responded the Colonel, he appreciated the question and was evidently expecting it.

"But how can I help?" Louis asked almost quizzically. "What particular requirement do you have of me that could possibly assist Mr van Rijn?"

At this point van Rijn stood to his feet again and walked to the window, looking out over the grounds to the back of the house. Rain had started to patter against the window sill. Outside the sky had become very overcast, yet inside the roaring fire kept the room illuminated.

Van Rijn looked to the floor, Louis sensed there was an ashamedness in the demeanour of the Dutchman.

"You have heard my dear friend the Colonel so eloquently describe the last twenty five years of my life gentlemen," began Marco van Rijn. He slowly turned back towards his audience. "However, what is missing is why I chose the path I did." Louis was not looking forward to this. Until now he believed there was uniformity in their mutual existence. He now sensed though that unlike himself, Mr van Rijn had been driven to his 'madness', for Louis it had simply been a natural progression.

"In nineteen forty the Nazis invaded my country," van Rijn lamented. "The true extent of their systematic raping of Holland has constantly been ignored. For political reasons the State has tried to dampen the truth of the harsh years under occupation. This was due to the desire of the bureaucrats to show appeasement throughout Europe. But do you know Mr Blue that only one in ten Jews survived the occupation in my country?"

Louis looked to his feet, he would not show emotion.

"My family," van Rijn continued, "had for many years enjoyed an particularly comfortable life, we were extremely fortunate. Our house was situated on the outskirts of Amsterdam. In nineteen forty, for the previous twelve months our lives had been thrown into turmoil with the savagery of what we could see going on all around us, everything we knew or loved was being destroyed. We lived a good life before the war, we had many friends and I always believed that we could rely on them through those dark days, that was until a family secret was revealed to the Nazis, for that we soon paid."

Louis appeared completely enthralled as the story unfolded, he was never one for fiction and in fact would rarely have any desire to read, his experiences he believed were far greater than any novel. He doubted whether there had there ever been a book that was as terrifying as his own experiences. Nevertheless he seemed drawn into the narrative.

"You see, my family, the van Rijn are descended of the miller's son from Leiden." Louis expression remained static. Van Rijn realised he would have to be a little more obvious.

"I am a descendant of the artist Rembrandt van Rijn." Louis raised an eyebrow, his interest in art matched that of his desire for reading, however he was aware that his shortcomings for the arts should not be allowed to overshadow the moment.

"Amazing," Louis responded, grasping the opportunity.

"Quite so Mr Blue, my ancestor's life had many ups and downs, much like us all. In his life he had enjoyed both riches and relative squalor, during one of these darker times he had been declared bankrupt. As a defence to both the effect and the requirements of such fall from favour, he took steps to ensure protection. Many of his unknown pieces were stored secretly where only his mistress knew. Everyone at some point has cast their eyes on a Rembrandt, whether it be The Mill or The Night Watch or The Supper at Emmaus. These paintings that showed both the majesty and failings of people captured both body and soul. For over three hundred years my family had been the guardians of these treasures, they belonged to us, entrusted by lineage and it was for my family to do with them as we saw fit. There was always to be a time when they would in their entirety be put on display across all the great museums of the world. London and Pairs to name but two. Yet my family had never believed there to be a specific date, a 'right time' to allow others to witness such riches."

The Colonel moved towards Louis, caught in the moment Louis had emptied his glass with particular haste. The Colonel duly topped it up.

Van Rijn continued. "Alas the opportunity to decide was taken away from us. Not only did they remove over ten hidden masterpieces, they also murdered my wife." He hesitated for a moment. "She was Jewish."

The atmosphere in the room suddenly chilled, even the fire's roaring flames seemed to appreciate the need for stillness. It was obvious to Louis, that the telling of such personal tragedy still greatly distressed van Rijn, not only had his family's honour been stripped, but it appeared from the grief brought on from his own recollection, that he had also had his heart torn out. Minutes later as the mood began to lighten a little, Louis sensed that eyes were starting to fix upon him. He now knew that his involvement in this tale was about to elevate from one of ardent listener to active participant.

Marco van Rijn had by this point fully composed himself. "My darling wife of course I will never be able to bring back. Regrettably, I believe that is beyond even you Mr Blue. However, the pieces of art can be recovered and I am in no doubt that you will be able to help me."

Louis was slightly taken aback by this comment. He didn't want to demonstrate too strongly, as this would reveal his ignorance of the world of art, but he really did struggle to see how on earth the men with him in this room could possibly believe for one moment that he could actually help at all, never mind return the treasures to van Rijn. Maybe somewhere along the line he had either said or done something in a previous mission that could have perhaps given others the impression that should you ever lose a painting Louis Blue was your man. Art detective was something he felt safe he could leave off his list of achievements to date.

"Gentlemen, sir, whilst I wholeheartedly sympathise with your loss on both counts, I fail to see how you believe I am the man for this particular task," Louis remarked. "You are all aware of what I do and how effectively I do it, but I cannot imagine why you think that my skills can be used to help return your lost paintings."

The Colonel smiled, "Of course Louis, if it had been a simple matter of locating the artwork in some obscure museum or private collection, then I'm sure Marco could quite easily go through the same systematic bungling process of trying to reclaim his collection that so many individuals have tried since the War and failed to achieve. There appears a reluctance of both public and private institutions to return what is so obviously not theirs. However, you are indeed correct, for that job I can think of no more unlikely a candidate than you Louis,"

Louis grinned, he knew his cover had been blown. Any attempt from this point on to represent himself on any level as being knowledgeable about art would have been an utter waste of time.

The Colonel continued, "However Louis, as you are maybe aware following the end of the War, many Nazis disappeared to the four corners of the globe and with them went much of the spoils from the countries they had occupied. Over the years, as a result of their desire to reclaim the eminence they had once enjoyed, many of the high ranking officers who had not been either killed, executed or arrested, used these prize assets to bargain their way back into society. Under either the protection of, dictatorships and there are many examples of these, or perhaps and even more likely the globally represented criminal organisations. It therefore follows old boy that should the Rembrandts be in either set of hands, then simply walking up, knocking on a door and saying 'please Mr President may I have my paintings back?' will not only likely end up without success, but quite will also leave you with a very nasty hole in the back of your head."

Louis was now starting to realise the game plan. He had to find a bunch of paintings somewhere in the world, be requested to kill a President or two, steal the paintings and then transport them back to van Rijn.

"Will I have any assistance?" Louis asked looking at both the Colonel and Abel Harrington.

"Of course dear chap," replied Abel Harrington, "you'll have me behind you all the way."

Louis smiled, he knew that the true talents of Abel Harrington were probably evident to others, but to date Louis struggled to remember the last time when caught in a tight spot that the impeccable Abel Harrington had provided any form of assistance. His role was normally to pat him on the back, always seeming to act as a go between.

"No, I actually meant do you have any information as to where the paintings may be now?" Louis asked, trying to disguise the desperation following Abel's not so comforting offer of assistance.

"Yes," the Colonel replied. "For the last three years our agents have been able, when time has allowed, to do a little work *pro bono*, so to speak. We have managed to piece together a rather interesting perspective of where and with who, much of the world's lost art treasures are presently located. Perhaps most interesting of all, is that some of the recipients are in fact well heeled members of established circles. That however is a different story and I am in no doubt that at some time in the future they will receive their comeuppance."

Louis' curiosity for a moment centred on who these individuals might be, but as he was not exactly a great player in society's social circles, he very quickly satisfied himself that even if names were provided at this point, he would be none the wiser.

"Louis, we expect you to begin work immediately on this project," barked the Colonel. Over the past several minutes he had glanced at the antique time-piece on the mantle-piece above the fire, Louis was in no doubt that the Colonel was most likely running late for some anniversary luncheon nearby with his old army pals. "The young lady that let you in, her name is Miss Sarah Caitlin, she has all the available files. I've instructed her to provide you with full access to everything. All I ask is that you give this your utmost care and attention. I appreciate you are not driven in the same way was as most Louis, but as I told you earlier, we owe Marco a lot. As a result you will be rewarded handsomely for your success with this project. Now we must away. You will keep us updated periodically as to your movements. Good luck Louis, we shall meet again soon, of that I have no doubt."

The Colonel and van Rijn left the room together. Abel Harrington walked to the window and sighed. "No rest for the wicked old boy," he said with a smile.

"No, how right you are," Louis responded, appreciating the utmost sincerity in the statement.

Sarah Caitlin entered the room carrying files under both arms. Louis immediately noticed two things, firstly, the files had the standard 'Top Secret' embossed across them all and secondly Sarah Caitlin was a very beautiful lady. It was the second observation that focussed Louis' attention. The regimented civil service attire apart, she most certainly appealed to Louis. He was loathed to remember the last time he had looked at a woman, never mind in a way that acknowledged her beauty. All too often the only time Louis would have reason to stare upon a female form was when it was lying at his feet deceased. This was the nature of the job and he had given up thinking about the target a long time ago , no matter male or female. Yet he was attracted to her beauty and this was quite frankly a feeling he rather enjoyed. Perhaps it was the whisky, he hadn't considered that.

She sat down at the table on the left hand side of the room and waited for both men to join her. In a way not trying to betray her femininity she removed the clip from her hair and a mane of long dark silky hair fell over the back of the chair. There were senses being aroused in Louis that were both unusual and pleasurable in equal quantities. He noticed her slightly olive skin, she had a Mediterranean appearance and her green eyes seemed to compliment the tanned complexion.

"Miss Caitlin, may I say what an honour it is to be working alongside you on this particular project." As her head turned and she fixed her eyes on Louis. He was immediately overcome with great shame and embarrassment. He believed he had just a made a complete fool of himself and no matter what happened from now on, he felt it better to just listen.

"Gentleman," she began, spreading the files across the whole table. "In the last eighteen months our agents have managed to infiltrate many global crime syndicates and some of the world's most volatile dictatorships. It pays to know where the next potential threat may come from. It is not always about the enemy that you can see, but sometimes about the one you don't know, the one that can plot and attack you without you expecting it. You read the papers and its not only the menace of communism that threatens our societies in the West. For example look at the way over the last few years drug-culture has taken hold. Behind this new vice there are criminal overlords that have influence at every level of both political and economic life. Their role alas is necessary in some countries as they are the infrastructure that keeps communism at bay. Whilst we don't condone the effect these people can have on society, we appreciate that all to often we have to support them, a kind of better the devil you know."

Louis had still not got to terms with the hatred of all things communist in the West. Much of his work had been carried out at the micro level to ensure there remained a status quo in the relationship between the two great global powers. He reckoned that nearly eighty per cent of his missions had been something to do with politics, but was it really that important that empires were being allowed to flourish based on crime, the absurdity of such a situation was plainly obvious to Louis.

Sarah Caitlin could see that Louis' mind had wandered. "Mr Blue," she looked directly at him, "As a result of the infiltrations we have attained a significant unexpected benefit, this being the potential finding of many stolen pieces of art. Till now these have been merely recorded and lucky we did, as we believe these records are going to make your task infinitely easier."

Louis felt a little more relaxed, he had no idea where he was going to start looking for lost paintings. The comments of the Colonel and the lady however had provided him with a little hope, that this task was not going to be as difficult as he had originally envisaged.

"One of the leading drug cartels based in Columbia has outlets all over the world. Much of their exports head directly into the United States through Mexico and then into California for distribution throughout the States. However, whilst this figure accounts for as much as seventy five per cent of all illegal drug exports, there is a growing global market with Europe being the outlet for much of this growth. Our information has highlighted a particularly nasty element in the Caribbean as a major centre for the receipt and provision of both drugs and laundered monies. Much of this is done right under the nose of the authorities without anyone being the wiser.

We thought it best to allow this to continue without any parties knowing of our involvement. We have to be sure that when we move to destroy these pipelines that we are not inadvertently throwing the country into political instability, yet also, we need to understand just how far the roots of these organisations have spread."

"Do you know much about this particular organisation?" Louis asked.

"Actually we believe we do," Sarah Caitlin responded, " as many do, this particular syndicate have managed to hide themselves behind a business with what would appear to have a very respectable front. Have your heard of Maradine Industries before? They are based on the outskirts of George Town on the Island of Grand Cayman. They are one of the largest manufacturers and distributors of prescriptive medicines throughout the whole of South America. They have managed to acquire sole distribution rights in many of the poorest South American countries. However, our information suggests they do this through either death threats or bribery of those in positions to agree such licenses. In many instances we believe this may even include Presidents."

Louis was not at all surprised, on three occasions he had reason to find himself in South America, twice in Argentina and once in Chile. On each visit he had witnessed first hand the degree to which dirty politics had managed to infest itself. If there had been a silver lining, it was by the time he had left the country one particular infested root had been removed.

Sarah Caitlin continued with her overview of Maradine Industries. "We have witnessed over the last twelve months the developing of operations in Europe, these activities are at present still very small, in fact in most countries they are still going through the process of obtaining acceptance certificates from the authorities. We believe that through the acceptable front of the company, these applications will probably be in time successful. However, of more concern is the mode of distribution, under the guise of bona fide drug exports, these will actually be hard core drugs destined for major European cities."

Over the past few years Louis had observed from a distance the growth of the drug culture, notably the *hippies* with their mind-bending chemical tablets and marijuana. It had seemed on the face of it all very harmless, but the threat of a substantial influx of these particular drugs or perhaps even worse would cause immediate concern, Louis could see the logic and rationality in Western cultures being rightly alarmed.

"At the head of the company, its Chairman, is a man called Juan Pablo Morientes," Sarah Caitlin continued, "he would appear to have risen from relative obscurity over the last few years to a position unparalleled by many of his peers, the other drug barons. Even by their meteoric ascendancies, the speed upon which his star has risen has left many of our people wondering how. The one thing we do however know of Morientes is that he is a lover of fine art and that somehow he is using collateral to fuel his growth, several Gustav Klimt works known to be worth in the region of several million pounds publicly adorn his offices. It would not take to much of a stretching of the imagination to believe that in Mr Morientes we may have the present custodian of the paintings."

Pondering as to the relative ease with which the paintings had seemingly been found, Louis was nonetheless not in a position to question the information. It seemed a comparatively straight forward assignment. Ascertain where Juan Pablo Morientes was, threaten him with a gun to the head, find out where the paintings were, pull the trigger and that would be that.

"Mr Blue," she continued, "our most recent information suggests that Morientes is now based in Grand Cayman Island in the Caribbean. It's obvious to us that the global perspective is now his main focus and has therefore relocated himself to the Island to provide the necessary anonymity required to ensure its success. We believe if we pay Mr Morientes a visit at his Island home we will find what we want.

Sarah Caitlin pointed at a file as yet unopened. "In that file is a dossier on the man and all information we have on his present whereabouts, his daily routine and a plan of his house. Please spend the rest of today absorbing all the information Mr Blue, tomorrow we leave for Grand Cayman."

"We?" snapped Louis, he did find the lady extremely attractive and for the present was enjoying being in her presence, but he worked alone, he had always worked alone, he was a lone hunter. In the animal kingdom there are many examples of predators who work most effectively by hunting in packs, but a lone hunter or for that matter the hunted have senses sharpened by the nature of the hunt. Louis was no wolf, he didn't hunt in packs and he recalled all to well the number of times he had managed to escape situations by the skin of his teeth, a job that had an element of danger, could soon become downright perilous.

"Yes, Mr Blue of course. I shall pick you up at eight tomorrow morning, ensure you get plenty of rest. My instructions which you may also now consider yours are to not return empty handed."

Sarah Caitlin rose from her chair and walked to the door, Louis now ready to deliver his view on this folly fleetingly fixed his eyes on her figure as she departed. For some reason he became dumbstruck as the door closed behind her. He turned to Abel who had sat all this time listening intently. He was now grinning, perhaps he had been right all along, it wasn't only the Dutch number plate on the car after all that had grabbed Louis' attention as they entered the house.

"Listen Louis, my dear chap, it's been a long twenty four hours, you'll need some rest. They've prepared a couple of splendid rooms for us upstairs, how about we turn in for a few hours and we meet down here at nineteen hundred hours for a spot of dinner?" Abel Harrington asked the question not really knowing if Louis was in the mood for light socialising. He needn't have worried as Louis nodded in agreement. It was however the thought of a decent meal rather than any form of interaction that had convinced Louis.

Dinner that night was a quite affair, Louis as ever was fascinated by not only how on earth Abel Harrington had come across his dinner attire, but how come it came to fit so damn perfectly. He had seemingly arrived as empty-handed as Louis, yet here he was impeccably groomed and suited for a grand occasion. His thoughts immediately turned to just how often Abel would actually visit this house. Perhaps there were many Louis' brought in from the field to be provided with dangerous missions and as a result Abel was a frequent visitor, maybe even a permanent resident.

As it was, dinner came and went and both men retired to their rooms for the night, for Louis however this would not entail much sleep. With the files under his arm he made his way to his door, once inside he sat down on the bed and immediately began to make himself comfortable. The next few hours were crucial, he needed to fully engage himself as to the mission ahead, the potential pitfalls and more importantly a successful strategy. This standard procedure was not unusual on the eve of an assignment, however, on this particular night there would also be an added complication, he would also have to ensure his plans would make allowances his new partner.

At seven fifty eight the following morning there was a light tapping at his door. Louis had been sitting peering out of his bedroom window at the back of the house for almost two hours, darkness had become light and he had watched as the frosted ground began to attract the first rays of sunlight.

"Morning Mr Blue," Sarah Caitlin greeted Louis as he opened the door to his room.

"Please call me Louis, Miss Caitlin," he responded with an awkward smile, his last attempt at sincerity had almost broken him, he was damned if he was going to cross that line again.

"Fine, if you wish Louis, then you must call me Sarah."

The clumsiness he felt which had clouded his offer was quickly erased by her response. With that Louis grabbed the files and followed Sarah down the stairs to the waiting car. Abel Harrington was sitting in the front passenger seat reading a copy of The Times. The driver from the previous day sat awaiting the order to drive. Louis gave him a nervous smile, the bruising around his neck was now clearly visible.

As the car weaved its way through the winding Surrey country lanes, Louis continued to gaze at the profile of his new partner. She in turn gazed as intently into the files, providing herself with the same level of familiarity with the task in hand as Louis had done the previous night. Every so often she would turn to Louis and catch his eye. He would immediately respond by averting his stare into the distance through the front window. Sarah smiled, she was unaccustomed to the attention.

The car headed north to the western outskirts of London, half expecting the car to continue to bear a north easterly direction, Louis was pleasantly surprised as the car began to follow signs for Heathrow. To pass through a commercial airport was a rarity, though perhaps even rarer was an attempt to leave the country without the benefit of a disguise, thus avoiding the usual gaggle of enemy agents waiting ceremoniously at the arrival and departure gates hoping to spot an enemy of their State, departing upon a mission or returning from completion.

Louis need not have worried, the car entered the main terminal complex and at once turned into a side road.

There was a clearly visible sign denoting private access. They turned round towards the back of the terminal and the car slowly came to a halt right at the foot of the stairs leading up to the plane. A BOAC 707 destination Miami, Florida awaited them.

As they boarded the plane Sarah informed Louis that they would be flying alone, with only certain high ranking officials from both the US and the UK on board. BOAC had yet to be granted a service route direct to Miami. This particular flight was not on any schedule as there were very few people the respective authorities believed should know of its regular coming and goings. It had become a very effective way of transporting individuals between the two countries.

The three sat close together. There were plenty of seats as there were approximately only twenty other people on board. As the flight left the runway, Louis looked down onto the green fields below. For the first time in many years he had hoped that his stay in the relative security of England would be a protracted affair. As it was, in just over twenty four hours he found himself leaving on yet another assignment. He felt the same crushing feeling he had experienced many times before. He was little more than a paid circus animal, people appreciated him for what he did, but there it stopped. He was always at their beck and call.

As the plane touched down in Miami, Louis disembarked for the transfer. The warmth of the sun immediately cloaked him. The last few months had seen him on many assignments in the northern Soviet States. A warm sun had seemingly become a distant memory. His attire therefore betrayed a somewhat ill-planned vacation, a woollen v-neck hardly seemed to be the ideal uniform of the Caribbean, but there would be plenty of time to collect the necessary clothing for the stay upon arrival at the Island's capital, George Town.

A car awaited them forty yards away, as the three approached it from across the tarmac, Abel Harrington turned to Louis.

"Okay Louis, this is far as I go, my role is to provide assistance and back-up should you so need it. This is my address and a contact number where I shall be staying here in Miami. I can be with you in two hours if necessary. I would kindly ask you call me every third night and update me as to any developments. When you have located the paintings and completed your task, one of you call me and I shall ensure that your removal from the Island shall be immediate. Good luck the pair of you."

With that, Abel Harrington strode of in the direction of the terminal. Louis gave him one brief backward glance as he and Sarah boarded yet another small four-seater Piper. The use of a private plane on the face of it appeared to serve no great purpose, Louis considered the likelihood of them being expected as almost non-existent. Yet it did remove the need for commercial connections with their lengthy delays and cancellations. The need was left in even less doubt, when upon opening the small leather case on the passenger seat beside him he found clothing, the right size and far more suitable for their destination.

The flight took just under three hours to Owen Roberts Airport. They both quickly changed in their nearest respective rest room. They were now fully indistinguishable from any other couple on the Island, that is until they reached their hotel.

Since the nineteenth century British diplomats used the Blue Star hotel, Located in the heart of the town, it provided formidable luxury to many a five star traveller. It was obvious to Louis that this was a mission that was attracting somewhat more investment than his usual jaunts. As tempting as it was as they entered the hotel lobby to hold Sarah's free hand, he realised this may just be a little too much. She looked completely worn out. They hadn't rehearsed this bit and after all, it had been so many years since he had held any woman's hand, it would be somewhat of a shame to do it for purely cosmetic reasons.

As they reached the receptionist's counter, an attractive local girl greeted them with a warm smile.

"Hello and welcome to the Blue Star Hotel. My name is Marianne, if I can just take your names I'll get you checked into your room."

"Dr Stefan Symes and I am Miss Victoria Ventner, his assistant," Sarah immediately responded.

Several moments later Marianne confirmed their booking and passed them two keys.

"You have adjacent rooms, just as you requested," Marianne again smiled. "Will you be needing an early morning alarm call?" she asked.

"No, that will not be necessary," Sarah replied.

With both keys in her hand, Sarah walked to the lift at the other end of the lobby. As the doors shut behind them, the false smile that she had carried through the entire check-in was now replaced by a stern expression. She focussed her eyes above the doors as the dial rose up to the third floor.

"There you are," she said, "room three two four, I'm in three two five. I'll see you in the morning, seven thirty."

Louis smiled to himself as he entered the room. He had decided against holding Sarah's hand keeping his hands by his side and as a result saved himself further embarrassment.

Louis was woken by the sound of a car horn outside the window. He arose from the bed and took a look through the partially closed blinds. The sky was clear blue and there was a warm breeze entering through the open window. He took a shower, got dressed and decided to call upon his colleague in the next room. He gently tapped upon the door and waited several moments. He imagined or perhaps was hoping that Sarah would come to the door dressed only in one of the hotel's bathroom towels. After several minutes it appeared the room was empty. Louis' thoughts now turned to food, he turned and made his way to the lift. It was time for breakfast.

After having spent the next thirty minutes enjoying several cups of coffee, eggs and tropical fruit, Louis' attention reverted back to Sarah. He'd begun to wonder where she'd got to. Just a short walk to the north was Seven Mile Beach. Much of the literature that marketed the Island made several claims to it being one of the best beaches in the entire Caribbean. Perhaps she had gone there for a morning swim. He decided to return to his room. However, as he passed the reception he caught a glimpse of Sarah getting out of a taxi, She was dressed in casual training gear with a bag slung over her shoulder.

"Follow me." she ordered as she brushed past him. Louis turned and did as he was told, following her to her room.

"Listen Louis," she whispered as though there was someone in the next room listening to their every word. "Morientes is here, on the Island, I saw him this morning enter the offices at Maradine Industries. They're not far from here, let's hurry, I hope we're not too late." Louis was impressed by Sarah's endeavours. He had been concerned that she would be nothing more than excess baggage on a potentially perilous assignment, but till now she had been more than a useful aide. She had actually managed to this point to achieve somewhat more that Louis had, but Louis knew that the test of one's strength of character can only truly be judged in the face of adversity. Sarah was at present eager to succeed. She was playing out the role of 'super sleuth' impeccably, but if the mission was to not go according to plan and potential dangers became reality, he could only hope that her determination to date would, if necessary, be matched by other notable attributes, she would after all be more than likely called upon to exercise them.

It was just before lunch that the two found themselves sitting outside the offices of Maradine Industries. They were situated on the outskirts of a small industrial park to the east of the Capital. It was on the edge of a major road linking George Town with the other towns and ports and therefore well placed for distribution.

The pair had parked on a slip road beside a small park opposite the main gates. After leaving the hotel they had deemed it prudent to hire a car. The Island is not extensive and taxis were abundant, but the distance to Morientes' house from the city was quite a ride. In addition, they had no idea for how long they may find themselves sitting and waiting. Therefore a small Ford was enlisted to assist the mission.

They parked the car facing the gate. Fortunately, it was innocuous given the number of other vehicles on the road.

The building itself was quite substantial, probably capable of accommodating more than five hundred staff. To the front and left of the building was a car park and to the centre right stretching round to the back of the complex was an ornate landscaped garden. There were palm trees lining the main drive down to the steps leading to what appeared to be the main reception. Whether legitimate or not, things were obviously going well for Maradine Louis thought.

The midday sun was beginning to make the pair feel somewhat uncomfortable inside the car. There was an old fan attached to the main dashboard and whilst it provided only a mild cool breeze it was welcome nonetheless. There was also a strip of tinted tape across the top of the windscreen. This was sufficient to almost completely hide the appearance of both occupants, but then the car was approximately two hundred metres from the main gates and therefore as a result, also the several security guards sitting outside their office. On the face of it the only occurrence that may alert this particular group of guards would be if the car actually ignited in the increasing heat, but even then Louis imagined, this would be unlikely to achieve anything more than a tertiary glance. The companions were safe where they were.

"What do you know of me?" Louis asked, shocked at the directness of his own question. This was alarmingly bold, especially as over the last few days any attempt at trying to bring himself closer to Sarah had resulted in a certain degree of embarrassment.

With such precedent he was hardly surprised by the equally direct response. "Nothing, why should I?" This statement had stunned Louis into silence, he nodded, not allowing his external expression of agreement to betray what he really thought.

After several uncomfortable moments Sarah turned in her seat to face Louis, "Look Louis, I probably know more about you than you do yourself. Do you think the department employs any Tom, Dick or Harry?" Louis' mind immediately focussed. It had been a great shock two days earlier to find he was part of some great communal agency. To be reminded that there were others like him had re-ignited the anger. She continued. "I have no idea where you were born, or who you really are. But there are many things I do know. For example, you have no idea why you were employed by the department. I do. You have no idea why you were truly selected for this assignment. I do and yes, I am fully aware that you find me attractive, as I do you, but we are on an assignment and I for one have no intention of failing this mission." With this she turned back to facing the guards.

"Women!" Louis whispered rolling his eyes, They both smiled.

In truth Louis had been completely taken aback by the outburst. It had been both bitter and sweet. The compliment had been totally unexpected. He was unused to such expressions of admiration, save the young ladies that commented upon passing when in recent months he'd been tasked with a mission in both Thailand and several weeks later Paris. But their offerings of praise had financial undertones. This was not Louis' want nor wish. He had in his sober moments regarded such comments as only relevant to those who were capable of emotion, cared or had an ego. As the he felt incapable of the first two and the only ego he had was of a professional nature, the words were often wasted. But from time to time, they brought him a little respite and whilst never reacting he was often inwardly thankful. The comments though from Sarah were different, they had a struck a chord. There was no denying it, but it was not that aspect of what she had said that had so impacted upon Louis.

Over the last two days, Louis had, more than ever before, begun to focus on who he was. His curiosity had been fired by the meeting with the Colonel and Marco van Rijn, but now following Sarah's revelations, his desire to find out more infuriated him. He had always been happy with the fact that at times he was a stranger even to himself. That was acceptable when he was safe in the knowledge that whilst he neither truly knew or cared to remember little, there would of course be no one who knew any more of him than he. To now be confronted with this was as shocking as it was interesting. He turned to Sarah.

"Listen you'll no doubt tell me you've already said to much, but when this mission is over, will you please tell me what you know of me?" Louis asked, desperately attempting to hide the angst in the question. There were episodes in his formative years that were simply missing. This at times could be comforting, but in equal measure there were times when the period of frustration of not knowing or being able to understand how one had arrived in a particular place was almost overbearing.

"You're of course right," she replied, "I've said to much already." Louis again nodded and turned back into his seat. He would have to wait.

As the clock beside the speedometer ticked towards four o'clock, the pair could feel the stifling heat from the sun starting to diminish. The temperature for a time had been almost unbearable. They were still acclimatising, but despite the distance and the apathy of the guards, they had felt it best to remain in the car and await developments. There was no point in taking any chances by alerting unwanted attention. At that very moment the gates began to slowly open. Both shot up in their seats. The gates had only opened on only a few occasions during the day. The car park to the left of the offices was outside the security fence perimeter, as was the distribution plant on the other side of the road from the car park. It was evident to both Louis and Sarah that the main drive up to the reception was for either very important visitors or high ranking dignitaries within the organisation. On this occasion however, the car, a stretch limousine entered and drew up near the front reception.

"That's the car I saw Morientes in this morning," Sarah stated her observation with an obvious excitement in her voice.

"Okay," replied Louis, "let's see what happens."

After several minutes of standing motionless, peering through one of the windows at the top of the reception steps, three men left the building, passed through the revolving doors and descended to the waiting car below. It was still too far away for Louis to ascertain who they were looking at. This, they realised would not be possible until the limousine drove back out through the security gate, but given Sarah's sighting in the morning, both were very hopeful that at last they could get moving.

They needn't have worried. As the car sped out past the saluting guards, an open window had yet to be closed as the car began to accelerate onto the main highway. This provided Louis and Sarah with a much closer view of who was inside. The man in the rear seat looking out almost directly towards them was Juan Pablo Morientes. A man of fifty two years of age, short with long greying hair tied back in a ponytail. He had the archetypal appearance of a typically affluent South American. He was impeccably groomed, his attire denoting his investment in his appearance. He looked like a man satisfied with life and all its pleasures.

Louis slammed the car into gear and they shot forward. He had done this many times before. It was imperative that he remained close but hidden. The latter was not going to be the problem. It was the remaining close that was causing an issue. The limousine darted through the traffic using its powerful engine to unknowingly lengthen the distance between them and their pursuers.

Sarah seemed far more concerned with Louis' driving skills than actually losing the car up ahead. "Relax," she shouted across to Louis. " We know where he lives anyway."

For almost an hour the cars continued in an easterly direction, through the town of Savannah and onto Bodden Town. The limousine came to a halt in the town centre. It was the old capital of the Island and it was here that the links with Britain were most evident in the street names and the prominent landmarks, such as the monument to Queen Victoria. Whilst other Islands and most notably Jamaica had been granted independence from Britain, Cayman chose to remain a Crown Colony. The Islands themselves were governed by an administrator who in turn reported directly to Westminster. As ever, this was a comfort particular to Louis. He would often spend months, sometimes years away from England. As a result, the England he knew and in truth felt most at home in was found in the many different outposts that had once defined an Empire.

In keeping then with the Victorian conservatism associated with many colonies, this town had a very relaxed, almost tranquil feel. If it were not for the need to keep their eyes focussed on the car ahead, parked by the side of small row of offices, they would have perhaps enjoyed the picturesque surroundings a little more.

Louis was tempted to bring the car in a little closer, however just as he restarted the car, one of the men got out of the limousine, he placed a parcel in the doorway of one of the shops and then calmly walked slowly back to his car. Once inside, the car departed, a little faster than they had travelled on the way to the town. Louis hit the accelerator, the car lurched forward, moving towards the pursued a little quicker than they actually anticipated, as first, the limousine, followed by the small Ford drove up a small incline. Just as the second car reached the brow of the slope, there was an almighty blast from behind them. The shop that had received the parcel was now a burning inferno. People were lying on the pavement outside what remained of the row of shops. It was likely, given the size of the explosion that there were many dead. Louis guessed it had probably been a payback for outstanding protection monies, or maybe a budding competitor. In fact without knowing too much about Morientes, it would be very hard to know why this act had actually been carried out. But one thing was for sure, this particular person had no concerns about killing, not the usual characteristic of an 'art lover'. Louis realised he might have to be a little more careful that he had previously imagined.

The small map they had brought with them proved useful over the next part of the journey. They could see from the small villages that they were heading north. They travelled to the east of the Little Sound Bay and on towards Rum Point. They passed several notable gated homes, all substantial in size. It didn't take much for Louis to imagine what it would be like to live in one of them. As a result, both Louis and Sarah had become distracted. As they looked back towards the road, to their horror the car had seemingly disappeared.

"Over there," Sarah called, pointing to a driveway bearing off to the right. The car had come to a stop outside a large iron gate. It was of course to be expected given the level of security at the plant and the two heavies that had accompanied Morientes in the car, that there should be no reason whatsoever to expect they could merely waltz in his home and take the paintings. No, the information held on file and the evidence of the last several hours suggested they could expect this home to be well guarded.

They drove for a further half a mile and parked the car. There was nowhere more suitable than behind a row of trees off the main road. They had now the advantage of failing light. This would allow them over the next hour or two to position themselves safely. From that point Louis could then move forward. He had no problems with Sarah's company to this point, but once at the wall he would go on alone. It would be impractical and also dangerous for them to enter the grounds together. They would wait until they reached the outer perimeter and were set to move into the house before he told her.

They stopped a couple of hundred metres short of the entrance to the grounds and decided to head through the woods on their left. They reckoned this would bring them right to the outer fence.

"Listen Louis, I think it would be a much better idea if you do this bit on your own," Sarah offered this with a slight degree of faltering in her voice. Louis was unsure as to whether this was fear on her part or whether she had realised that at this stage, the success of the actual theft would be far more likely if Louis entered the house alone rather than having to look after her too.

Louis waited for the last remains of sunlight to depart the sky. The was now an eeriness to the evening. The only sound audible from their position were the crickets in their close vicinity. There was also the distant drone of the occasional car passing by on the small road. Louis turned to Sarah and held out his hand. One of the principal benefits of not passing through commercial airports is that by avoiding customs and the various layers of passport security you can bring almost anything into a country. Sarah reached into her pocket and pulled out a Smith and Wesson model sixty. Louis had been expecting the standard Heckler and Koch, yet now was not the time to turn back based on the availability of preferred weapon. When he had been informed that all necessary essentials would be provided, he hadn't deemed it necessary to actually go into any great detail as to what his specifications were. Sarah also passed him a standard hunting knife with serrated edges. This was a standard issue. It could be easily concealed, made no noticeable noise as it was exercised and could be conveniently carried without arousing to much suspicion. Explaining the need for a knife was always somewhat easier for Louis to explain than that of a gun whenever stopped and searched.

The visible security around and within the house was evident, although not excessive. Fortunately for Louis the sea breeze coming in from the coast was less than a quarter of a mile away. There was a noticeable wind blowing in their direction. This would cloud any scent that patrolling guard dogs may have picked up. Yet that would be taking chances. Louis decided to come in from the eastern side of the house, therefore, should any of the dogs have a particularly sensitive nose, by going to the furthest point to the east he would substantially increase his chance of success .

Louis gave an acknowledging nod to Sarah and clambered up over the fence, following it round to the western side of the house. He dropped down into a small ditch, took several deep breaths and then shot forward to a tall palm tree on the other side of a wide open clearing. Sarah was watching his advance all along. There appeared to be no dogs, but she could see imminent danger on the opposite side of a small lagoon. Guards silhouetted against the internal lights of the house were continuing their rounds. This was bringing them directly towards Louis. Within two minutes they would be upon him. As the guards approached the lagoon, both Sarah and Louis could see there were four guards in total walking the grounds pairs. One pair walking the grounds in a clockwise and the other in an anti-clockwise direction. As the pair threatening the most obvious danger moved towards Louis, they parted at the lagoon, one deciding to follow the edge of the lagoon back round towards the house and the other continued on a collision course with his impending fate.

Louis had turned and leant with his back resting against the tree, facing out in the direction he had just approached from, he was now relying on his hearing to guide him. The footsteps were getting closer and closer. The small pathway would bring the guard to within two feet of the tree Louis was using as cover. Louis waited until the sound of the heavy boots on the ground indicated that the guard was almost upon him. He broke from the tree and with a jab directly to the throat, burst the knife straight through and out the other side of the man's neck. Physical inability aside, the guard just stood rooted to the spot. He had been staring into the water as Louis pounced. With great force, Louis pulled the blade back, tearing and ripping as it returned. Within an instant he had forced the blade through the front of the scull and punctured the brain. The guard fell to his knees. At least he had been eliminated by a professional, one of the best, Louis thought. Unless required, enduring pain was seldom the way for his victims and equally in turn Louis seldom felt pity. On this occasion there was no question of compassion, the guard had an ugliness and mean perspective to his face. Louis considered that undoubtedly somewhere there would be a bereaved family for who he had just enacted his own particular method of revenge.

Louis slid the body into the water, ensuring it made no splash as it entered. The body immediately sank. He had no concerns though, the lagoon was not lit and even if the body was to float Louis reckoned he would be either long gone or long dead by the time either it surfaced or the sun rose.

He moved on towards the house, following the path round the water's edge. He had no idea how many, if in fact any guards were within the residence. Thankfully, the layout on the ground floor level had no blinds or any noticeable form of shade. With much of the house at that level open plan, he figured that if there was in fact anyone in the nearby, they must be on the upper levels. He had also still to determine how he was to get the paintings away. He soon realised it would pay to do all he could to ensure that there were as few guards as possible to contend with on fleeing from the house. Louis would try and take care of the second of the first pair of guards who had approached him as he came back round the lagoon. Louis reckoned this would give him at least another thirty minutes until the second pair returned. Louis climbed up into the tree beside him and lay prostrate on a large branch approximately three metres from the ground. He again decided to rely on his acute hearing to tell him when to strike. He looked calmly up at the stars and waited. The steps became louder until they were almost below him. As he sensed the guard beneath him he dropped a twig behind the guard, the guard turned as the twig hit the ground. At that moment Louis swung upside down, his legs wrapped around the branch. In a movement resembling a pendulum Louis allowed the momentum to carry the knife right into the upper spine of the man. With one final twist of his hand, the spinal chord was severed and the man crumbled into a ball on the floor. The action was executed in a matter of seconds. Thankfully Louis realised that from her position Sarah was unable to see any of this. It was not something he would wish for her to witness.

Louis' access to the house was now relatively simple. He moved up to the main area behind the building beside the swimming pool. Using the protection afforded by the darkness he kept close to the floor. He needed to avoid being visible against the backdrop of the light from any of the rooms. Louis felt his way using his hand around the outer wall of the house, there were three sets of doors. All had been locked. By chance, he could see only a short distance away to his right there was an open window. On nearing the fortuitous break in the houses inner security, he could see that on the other side of the window lay the kitchen.

Louis gently lifted the window further, hoisted himself up on to the sill and twisted his legs up and through the opening. Within seconds he had jumped out over a large sink and was now standing in the middle of the floor. At that very instant the door to an adjoining room slowly turned. A young boy no older than ten entered and stood motionless, looking directly at Louis displaying no fear.

"Damn," Louis whispered through gritted teeth. He was not one for killing children unless it was absolutely necessary. The boy's silence relaxed Louis a little and therefore a calm began to overtake the tense situation.

"Don't say a word," Louis whispered to him. The boy looked again blankly, with no notable signs of fear but equally no visible signs that he was about to do anything to make worse an already deteriorating situation. It was most probably the son of Morientes, but it was the father Louis had come to see him and had no reason to kill his son. He therefore grabbed the boy and placed his hand tightly over his mouth. He lifted him and placing him under his arm retraced his steps, following exactly the way he had just come, back towards Sarah. He guessed she would know what to do with the youngster.

"That is most definitely not a painting," she whispered angrily to Louis as he passed the child over the fence.

He placed the knife in Sarah's hand. He believed it unnecessary to tell her what to do, for one, it was almost unimaginable that she would be able to bring herself to kill him and secondly he had remained motionless since being grabbed by Louis. The trauma of the last two minutes had probably rendered the child incapable of panic and therefore unlikely to jeopardise the mission.

Louis repeated his original approach all the way back to the house and in through the kitchen window. He reckoned that perhaps the room from which the boy had appeared there could be others, maybe even his father. Louis slowly turned the handle on the door. It was the one room that appeared closed off from the outside. It was therefore impossible to tell what or who was inside from any approach to the house.

The door gently opened. Thankfully for Louis there was a rug on the other side of the door. This muted any potential scraping of the bottom of the door against wood or tile. He poked his head slowly in through the space the opening had provided, keeping his gun now very close to his face. Once inside, he peered around. It was a magnificent dining room It appeared to take up over fifty percent of the downstairs floor space. However, it struck Louis that what he was looking at was completely at odds with the rest of the house. There were extremely ornate carvings on the dining table and chairs. The table was capable of seating at least thirty diners at one sitting without a problem. One of the chairs was pulled out and several books in Spanish lay open. It was obvious the young boy was doing his homework when he'd entered the kitchen, probably for some refreshment.

It was not the furniture at ground level however that was now grabbing Louis' attention. On the wall down both sides and at the ends of the room, were hanging at least twenty paintings. Louis of course would have no idea who had painted them were it not for his mission. His logical assumption was that among them were the missing Rembrandts. If they were not all here, the others would be more than likely upstairs.

At the far end of the room were the main doors. They were large and made of oak panel. Having now outlined a layout of the ground floor in his head, Louis realised that these doors, when opened, were facing the windows at the front of the house. Time was running out. He had probably no longer than twenty more minutes before the alarm would be raised for either of the missing guards.

He opened the doors and instantly realised that anyone outside the front of the house looking in would see him clearly. He dropped to the floor and immediately appreciated that in order to remain hidden, he would need to crawl to the stairs to his left. They were two metres in front of him. Once at the stairs he straightened up and walked forward very carefully, with the gun poised in his right hand, he approached the landing.

The house was very well lit, whoever was responsible for the lighting had turned on nearly every light in the house. This did not make the task impossible, but it hardly helped. By now though there was no turning back, much of the hard work had already been done.

At the end of the corridor on the other side from where he was standing, Louis could hear a noise coming from behind one of the doors. He moved very slowly, on his toes, keeping his eyes focussed on every door as he passed, determined not be startled by an unexpected entrance for a second time that evening.

He arrived at the door to the room from where the noise appeared to be emanating.

Louis could now clearly hear the sounds of Latin music, he judged it to be emanating from a record player due to the occasional scratching noises intermittently breaking up the sound of the trumpets. Rather than the cautious approach, this time Louis turned the knob and thrust the door forward.

Lying on the bed dressed in a open shirt and underwear was Juan Pablo Morientes, he looked up at the intruder and moved for his holster slung over the end of his bed.

"Do not move or I will shoot you Mr Morientes," Louis said in a very calm manner. If only flirting with his colleague was as easy as threatening to kill a man. Morientes had his movements however checked by the young lady who was lying beside him on the bed, herself only wearing underwear. Panicked by the sudden intrusion, she ran straight for Louis, more than likely she was heading for the only exit, the door that Louis was standing in front of. As she approached, Louis knew he couldn't let her simply run out. Luckily her screaming was being drowned out by the high notes being reached on the trumpets. Louis reversed the gun in has hand and brought it crashing down on top of the girl's head. She would have a headache in the morning nothing more.

"Who are you American?" Morientes snarled at Louis.

"Actually Mr Morientes I'm," at that point Louis paused, how did he know himself where he came from, maybe a little implausible but although he sounded English it didn't actually mean he was English. If Sarah was here she may well have been able to answer the question for him. Assuming that Morientes wasn't also in on the secret and realising that this was not perhaps the best time to be pondering such issues, he responded.

"What or who I am is irrelevant, you have some things that I believe do not belong to you and I am here on behalf of the rightful owner to return them. Do you understand me?"

"Listen," Morientes replied almost immediately, "I do not know who you are or what you are doing here, but you and your family will die for this."

"Alternatively," responded Louis, "It will be you and your family who will die Morientes if I do not get what I came here for. We have your son and believe me, if I do not return in fifteen minutes, I will order someone waiting nearby to kill your son. Trust me, they will enjoy doing so." The threat to Louis' family was as irrelevant as it was unlikely. If he was actually aware of any family he may have been a little concerned for their safety, but he wasn't so the threat was therefore spectacularly redundant.

The man scowled at Louis and shook his head. Louis had now said enough to ensure that he now had Morientes' undivided attention.

"So again, Mr CIA what do you want?" Again ready to remonstrate with the man, Louis thought better of it, he could think of worse things to be called.

"Your paintings, the ones downstairs, where are the others?" demanded Louis.

"What others?" replied Morientes, "Apart from some local art, all of the treasured pieces are in the dining room. You came here for those?" Morientes chuckled. "Stupid man, not only are they almost incalculable in value, they are unique, how do you intend to hide them once you have gone?"

"Let me worry about that, now where are the others?" Louis was now beginning to become a little agitated. There was hardly time enough for one painting, how was he going to get them all out in the time he had left. "Downstairs quickly," he ordered Morientes down into the dining room, making him crawl the last few feet.

Once in the dining room, both men looked around. Louis remembered his visit to the Louvre in Paris the previous year. The layout and appearance of the room had a striking similarity.

"You are about to steal one of the finest collections of paintings in the world. You are a very brave man." This statement was not directed towards Louis for the purpose of providing a compliment, no, this had more the undertones of a direct threat.

"That over there, is a Klimt, alone it is almost priceless. It is of a young woman painted at the turn of the century. That one over there was painted by Salomon van Ruysdael in sixteen forty nine."

"Do not test my patience Mr Morientes. Which of these are Rembrandts?" Louis now realised his lack of knowledge in terms of art and in particular great paintings, had left him somewhat on the back foot. He was going to have to trust a megalomaniac drug baron to hand over priceless pieces of art by relying on him to identify which of the paintings were Rembrandts.

"I can assure you, none of these are Rembrandt. My supplier of such works of art shares my dislike of the Rembrandt. His paintings are a little too lifelike for my taste. I prefer something be left to the imagination. If you don't believe me, you need only look at the original signature at the bottom to denote who the artist is."

Louis leant forward, it was true, on the few he looked each had the artists signatures, nothing appeared to resemble a signature resembling a Rembrandt. This way not always the way to denote a master, but for Louis it was enough. He had the boy and Morientes was aware of that, It was unlikely, Louis reckoned, that he would risk the life of his son for some paintings, no matter who had bloody painted them.

"Tell me Morientes, If you don't have any of the Rembrandt paintings, where will I find them?"

"Have you tried looking in a museum? Idiot!" replied Morientes. He was now mocking Louis.

Louis, again turned the gun in his hand and this time smacked the butt of the gun across Morientes' nose. He fell to the ground, the blood poured across the floor.

"I will kill you and your son with ease Mr Morientes, I suggest you tell me now what I want to hear."

Morientes picked himself up slowly, using one of the chairs as a prop. He began to speak, although, with a broken nose and blood flowing down the back of his throat, this was always going to be a struggle.

"Truthfully, I do not have any of the paintings you are searching for here. I am, how shall we say, a keen enthusiast of the art of the Masters. I once heard of several missing Rembrandts, but the number you are searching for is far greater than anyone can ever have imagined. I truly wish you good luck. If you are successful, your achievement will be by far the greatest discovery the art world has ever witnessed."

"Okay, you tell me where to start looking and I shall let you and your son live." Louis by now was convinced that this was the truth. He could see it in his eyes, Morientes had too much to lose.

"The Chinese. Most of the pieces passed around in the black market are normally sourced through Hong Kong. You will need an army though Mr Whoever-the-hell-you-are. If you think you can win that battle alone, you are in for a very nasty surprise."

"Names, I need names." Louis by now was furious that amongst all of these fine pieces, there was not one that had any relevance, no relevance at least for this mention.

"The House of Scorpion. That is all I can tell you, as that is all that I know." At that moment Louis could hear noise from outside. The second pair of guards had either come across one of the bodies or else their disappearance had caused alarm. Louis had no time to waste. He turned and ran out through to the kitchen, out of the window and sprinted as fast as he could out towards the fence.

The guards were on the far side of the lagoon and house respectively. Louis made it with ease back to Sarah and the boy. After placing the boy back inside the security fence, they both turned and ran back to the car.

Louis turned the ignition and the car lurched forward. "For Christ's sake Louis, where are the paintings?" demanded Sarah,

"Hong Kong I believe," replied Louis with almost an air of nonchalance.

"What on earth are they doing there?" she immediately asked.

"I believe a scorpion has got them," came the response. The reply had meant as much to Sarah as it did five minutes earlier when Louis had first been told. "Best we get back to the hotel and get off this Island Sarah, there's no point us staying here any longer. I believe it to be highly likely our paintings are elsewhere," continued Louis. "When we get back to the room give Abel a call and arrange for our departure."

On the way back to the hotel Louis explained the events that had unfolded and the rather unusual reference to a scorpion. The concept of a criminal using an alias was not new to either of them. But in this instance the reference was vague. Louis wished he'd been able to extract a little more information about the 'House of Scorpion'. That hadn't been possible. Nevertheless, a positive was that they could now cross Morientes off the list and despite the fact that they were unsure as to what or who they were now looking for, Hong Kong was where the trail was now about to take them.

"Good evening Doctor Symes. Good evening Miss Ventner." Marianne greeted them both as they entered the hotel's reception. "Were you studying the fish today?"

Sarah turned to Louis and smiled. "Yes," he exclaimed, now fully understanding the cover story and why it had been given, it was perfect should their stay have been protracted for any unforeseen reason. "But they were a trifle disappointing Marianne, we've decided to focus our attention on Oriental fish. So alas I'm afraid were going to leave. Please provide us with our bills, we shall be departing imminently."

They both returned to their rooms for the ten minutes it would take for the taxi to arrive. A rather puzzled receptionist was busily putting together their bills whilst attempting at the same time to connect a call through to Miami.

Abel Harrington met them at the airport. He had a look of concern that was not only portrayed in his expression, but also in the way he hastened towards them.

"Oh dear, oh dear, such a shame. We were so sure we would find the paintings there. All our intelligence pointed to that very place." Abel frowned as he spoke.

Louis' response was as usual curt and straight to the point. "Well it would be fair to say that in this particular instance the intelligence was somewhat lacking." Both men knew only to well that the information normally supplied was never wrong. It was impeccable in it's degree of accuracy. To have been sent on a wild goose chase seemed to Louis almost unthinkable. Yet the facts were staring both men in the face. Someone had screwed up.

Several days later Louis and Sarah were back in London relating all that had been seen and all that they had learned. The somewhat odd reference to the 'House of Scorpion' had everyone bemused. For a department that believed that for every corner of the globe they had file upon file of intelligence on all the shadiest of characters and organisations, to suddenly find that in one of their own territories, there may be an individual or institution, acting either as a middle man or a home for some of the world's greatest lost masterpieces, would entail for someone somewhere some very embarrassing questions.

Their plane touched down seventy two hours later at Kai Tak Airport, Hong Kong. Louis was fascinated by the East. His many trips there had allowed him to experience such beauty seldom seen elsewhere. Yet in equal measure he had also witnessed first hand the barbaric treatment of other human beings. He puzzled at the paradox of how a people so focussed on the soul and the spirit, could without reason worship the sanctity of one's soul with such purity, but then in turn inflict such pain and torture upon their neighbour. He had found himself on several occasions in the rat infested prisons of Korea and Thailand. He was sure he had only descended thirty steps or so to his cell, but on each time he felt as though he had arrived in Hell.

His rationale for his actions were steadfast. He had no desire to worship his soul or anyone else's soul for that matter. He looked across to Sarah and smiled, he had either chosen to, or had somehow failed to appreciate how irrational was his thinking. This woman had been with him constantly for the last eight days, not that it mattered much if she hadn't, as she had never been far from his thoughts. Within a short time he had begun to feel a responsibility for her he never believed possible, but whilst he was becoming her protector and guardian, perhaps she, in such return had become his saviour.

Hong Kong to all who visited was a contradiction. A hustle bustle kind of city so typical of South Eastern Asia, but nonetheless retaining strong ties with its British colonial past. This was evident in the street names, the parks and the very way the people of Hong Kong went around their business. One could be easily imagine that the city was no more than fifty miles from London. Although somewhat warmer, it afforded a comforting outpost.

As they departed the airport complex they spotted a driver holding a sign. It read 'Dr. Symes & Ventner.' Realising the implausibility of such a coincidence, Louis walked directly to the car. He had always considered himself a solo operator, but from time to time the little annoying perspectives of operations such as taxis and hotels were for the large part taken care of. In addition, he always knew that somewhere in the shadows was Abel Harrington. Although unusually, he had not been on the plane, it also suddenly dawned upon him that he hadn't seen him for several days. He now realised the growing preoccupation of Sarah in his mind had resulted in an irrelevance to almost everything else. Louis just hoped that Abel's absence was either less significant than on other assignments, or perhaps more comforting, it indicated that he was already here, just waiting to emerge from some hidden doorway.

"Blue Star Hotel" the driver said looking at them both in the rear view mirror. Louis pondered for a moment. Few taxi drivers told the passengers where their destination would be, but yet the Blue Star chain of hotels appeared to have some form of departmental approval. Wherever assignments allowed and accommodation had been pre-booked, it was quite likely this particular chain would be chosen. There would always be substantial periods when other chains were used for security reasons, too much repetition would be foolish. But the Blue Star invoices would more than likely make up a substantial proportion of the department's 'mission expenses'. Louis had no qualm with that, the rooms were always comfortable and the people friendly.

"Louis, where do we start?" asked Sarah. "We have so little to go on and if we walk around asking does anyone know the House of Scorpion, we'll either end up being locked up in a madhouse or else we'll end up unknowingly bringing the 'Scorpion's sting' to us and that may be dangerous."

Louis nodded, "I agree, the reason we are here however is related to art. If we are to find the lost paintings there are several things to consider, perhaps the most obvious being the location of the House of Scorpion. Can we assume that this stolen art is best located through thieves or through artists?"

"That's an assumption Louis is it not?" replied Sarah, turning to him and smiling. "Can an artist not also be a thief?"

Louis appreciating the attempt by Sarah to provide a little humour to proceedings, replied. "Well given some of the rubbish you see hung in the museums and galleries around the world, I guess they can be." Louis had in the last ten years been to exactly the same number of museums as he had galleries. On both occasions he had been following a target. His statement therefore had no conviction and he appreciated that Sarah had realised this. Notwithstanding his weak attempt as humour, Sarah giggled at his response. Louis eased a little and relaxed back into the car seat.

Both had agreed to meet that evening at half past seven in the dining room. They requested a table in the corner beside the window. The humidity in Hong Kong was a little higher than had been expected for this time of the year, so the additional occasional light gust of air brought extra relief.

After a light meal involving mainly noodles and what appeared to be chicken. Louis rested his head in his cupped hands. "Right, tomorrow we go to City Hall, the Hong Kong Museum of Art is there, I can think of no better place to begin. It is advertised in one of the local guide booklets In my room, we'll start there."

They agreed to set off early. "If we leave at seven, it should still be relatively quiet." Sarah had not been to Hong Kong before. Her suggestion would make sense in most cities, but Hong Kong was very rarely quiet. Louis however was not prepared to suggest an earlier departure, they had no idea who or what faced them in the morning and therefore getting as much rest as possible would seem to make sense.

The streets by seven were, as expected, full of people. They decided to walk down Nathan Road with all its shops and little street sellers. At the end they took a stroll through Kowloon Park. The time was now half past eight. It would be another fifteen minutes before the doors opened.

They both sat down on a park bench, opposite an old man and woman who sat quietly at a table playing cards.

"Are you married Sarah?" asked Louis.

"No, have never really had the time to meet anyone special. You know how it is, married to the department and all that." Louis nodded in agreement with her statement, actually he had no idea, but he was pleased with the response nonetheless.

"Yes, of course," he replied, pleased not only with the reply but also that the question had almost been welcomed, "I hope you don't mind me asking, just passing the time, nothing else."

"No, of course not, anyway what about you Louis, have you ever been married?"

"I thought you knew everything about me Sarah, you must surely know whether I've ever been married."

"It's true, you're aware I know a great deal, not everything though, but you are quite right, I knew you weren't married, but I thought I'd ask anyway."

They both smiled. Flirting was not part of Louis' standard repertoire. He felt more at ease looking into someone's eyes as they struggled for their last mortal breaths, but this was something entirely different. He looked to the ground and blushed, unable to maintain eye contact.

Louis checked his watch. It was now ten to nine. He patted his knees and nodded towards the museum. They both arose, crossed the street and walked up the steps to the main door. An elderly lady smiled as they walked past her. Louis sensed that they would have to identify a curator as soon as possible, as enticing as strolling through a museum enjoying Sarah's company seemed, they were on a mission and nothing else should matter.

The museum appeared to be a fusion of Western and Eastern influences, although on examination, there was indeed a far greater oriental feel to the exhibits. There was a great deal of ornaments which was hardly surprising given the close proximity to China. The section designated to paintings was in a large room with high ceilings but with very few windows, minimising the amount of natural light. Covering the walls were paintings of all sizes, the majority, explosions of very bright colours. Louis was no expert, but it didn't take him long to realise that the paintings on show here were a little different from those found in the museums of London, Paris, Rome and New York.

"May I help you?" Sarah jumped, she had been taken by surprise by the little man who had seemed to appear from nowhere.

"I am Mr Li, I am the one of the guides for the museum and if there is anything you may wish to know, then please, just ask me and I will endeavour to answer you."

Like many educated local people in Hong Kong, there was an air of imperiousness about this little man. He stood no higher than Louis' chest, had grey hair slicked back and a smile that seemed almost frozen to his face. The look combined with his silent approach had somewhat startled Sarah and she had found herself moving slowly away, putting Louis between herself and what she now considered to be a sinister dwarf.

"Thank you indeed Mr Li," replied Louis. My name is Dr Symes and this is my assistant Miss Ventner. We are marine biologists, but we also have a passion, although somewhat amateurish, for art. Tell me, most of the paintings here seem to represent the locality of the region, I was hoping to see some of the great master's classical pieces there, do you have any such works on show at present?"

"Ah, Dr Symes, what an interesting individual, you have a passion for both nature and art and you travel with a beautiful woman. You are indeed a very lucky man." Sarah squirmed as Mr Li looked her up and down as he delivered the compliment. "Please follow me, both of you, down the stairs at the back of the hall. We keep our most treasured pieces there, they are there for additional security."

All three walked briskly towards the far end of the room and proceeded to descend the stairs. Mr Li took a small set of keys from his waistcoat, opened the door and beckoned both Louis and Sarah to follow him into the room.

Once into the dark room, Mr Li began to close the door with all three of them now inside.

"Tell me Dr Symes," Mr Li began to speak as the door was now shutting, "how are you finding the weather here in Hong Kong, a little more comfortable than the Caribbean perhaps?"

The reaction from Louis was immediate, his skills were honed, within a fraction of a second his leg coiled and then exploded in both the direction of the little man and the door. His foot contacted with the chest of Mr Li who crashed against the door, it swung open with the impact. In fact it was nearly taken off its hinges as it thudded against the outer wall.

"I would advise you to stop immediately Dr Symes." Louis spun round. Instantaneously a very dim light was switched on. At the end of the room, a large Chinese man had his arm around Sarah's neck and was holding a knife to her temple. There were two others of a similar size standing either side of him, yet Louis was unsure which of them had offered the advise.

"So Dr Symes, are you going to tell me who you both are and what your are doing here, or am I going to have to kill your lovely assistant?"

Louis immediately turned to the far corner of the room, it was hidden in the shadows, but Louis could just about make out the outline of a very tall man.

"I am here with my assistant to look at art, why have you done this to us?" replied Louis.

"Oh come come Dr Symes, please do not play games with me. Whether innocent or not, I will have no qualms in killing you both, so please, let us cease with this foolishness now and tell me why you are here. I am aware of your recent trip to Grand Cayman. You will soon learn that I am not the sort of person you come looking for Dr Symes, for I will always find you first. That fool Morientes should not have mentioned me, for the sake of that tiresome child he gave you my name and now alas they are both are no more."

Sarah froze, the thought of Morientes having been killed was not so regretful, in fact she was sure the world would be a safer place with such an evil man gone, but the child's death made her feel sick. He had looked so innocent and ill-prepared for the events of the other evening. To think that someone with such little compassion had been able to murder him too had now helped convert her sadness into anger, this in turn was helping her cope her present dire situation.

Louis walked towards the shadow, however his path was blocked by one of the large other men who moved forward, he was holding a pistol in his hand. Louis stopped and retreated a couple of steps.

"I'm after some paintings. I was led to believe that Morientes could help me. He couldn't, but he gave me your name." Louis addressed his response in the direction of the shadows.

"Listen Dr Symes, the one thing I can be completely sure of, is that under no circumstances would a doctor turn up at the home of Morientes, threaten to kill him and his son and then travel to the other side of the planet, more than likely using a alias in doing to so.

"I love art," Louis' response was as sarcastic as it was obviously a lie.

Sarah groaned as the grip around her neck tightened and her captor applied more pressure with the blade against her temple.

"Dr Symes or whoever you are, this is your final warning. You must tell me now who you are and what you are doing here."

"Okay, let her go," Louis responded to the warning. He could see that this was no hollow threat. The death of Morientes and his son had demonstrated that they were more than capable of carrying this through. "I have been employed by a very wealthy individual to locate, offer then purchase some lost masterpieces."

"Really, now that sounds very interesting, please continue Dr Symes." The man in the shadows took a couple of small steps forward. Again Louis could not identify the man's face but could easily make out the outline of his features. Whilst not clear, he could see that the man was of Western appearance, not Chinese.

"But, I was led to believe by Morientes that you did not intend to purchase any paintings Doctor, rather your intention was to take some paintings without paying." The tall man chuckled, perhaps at the audacity of the attempted heist or maybe because he had found a flaw in Louis' story, either way Louis had no intention of backing down.

"That was a genuine misunderstanding." Louis spoke with a growing confidence. "I doubted I would be granted an audience and therefore decided to invite myself to the house. I was discovered, Morientes was startled and the confrontation arose from that. Listen, my instructions are clear, I am to return with some missing Rembrandts. That's all I know and all I'm prepared to tell you. I believed from what Morientes told me, that you would have them here in Hong Kong and would be prepared to sell them to me."

"Well then that is why he is dead, but you refer to the missing Rembrandts?" The man's head turned to the side. Louis guessed that his comment had genuinely caught him by surprise. " I am aware of the odd one or two, but any more than that I believe must be a myth. For those that I know to be in existence, are never truly missing, it's just, how shall I put it, circumstances have resulted in the owner suddenly mislaying them. Yes, from time to time

I find myself distributing some of the world's finest art treasures to true connoisseurs, for that I take my cut. In turn that has also allowed me to grow my own little private collection, which is now worth many millions of dollars, but tell me, how many missing Rembrandts do you believe there are?"

"Ten" replied Louis.

The man began to laugh. " You are a very funny man, now stop wasting my time, any more foolish comments and this conversation will be the last one you ever have. Now tell me again how many paintings is your buyer looking for?"

Louis could tell from the response that either he was an extremely gifted actor or it was highly unlikely that he knew of the ten paintings. The amusement that the suggestion of their existence had caused provided Louis with immediate affirmation, this was not where the paintings were.

"Tell me, Scorpion," Louis paused for a moment, "I presume that's your name?"

"You may call me that." responded the man.

"If I was to ask you to sell me some Rembrandts, how many would you be able to provide me with assuming that money be no object?"

"If money were no object and that is a very big "if" when referring to Rembrandts, then I would say perhaps two maybe three, but that would take time and your client would require very deep pockets."

"Trust me, my client is a very wealthy individual," Louis responded, sensing that the atmosphere was becoming a little less tense and that perhaps an opportunity to escape now existed.

The man walked from out of the shadows, he beckoned the men standing either side of Sarah and the large man with a vice-like grip around her neck to bring the chairs to the wall at the far side of the room. They placed them underneath the light bulb. Louis had a small table to his left and moved towards it, realising very quickly that The Scorpion was first and foremost a businessman and could see a very significant opportunity arising.

The Scorpion emerged from the shadows. " We can discuss your proposal Dr Symes," he nodded in the direction of the table. Sarah felt the grip around her neck begin to ease, now able to breathe freely, she took some exaggerated long breaths.

"Are you okay?" Louis asked, placing his hand on her shoulder.

"Yes, yes, I'm fine." Sarah lied. She was petrified. Her training and her skills had not prepared her for this. She had expected excitement but this was a little too real. Her fear was beginning to paralyse her, she wanted to make a rush for the door, but yet, there was something inside her that took courage from the calmness being demonstrated by Louis. He appeared to be completely relaxed, as at ease with this situation as he had been a few minutes earlier when walking around the museum.

All three were now sitting around the table under the dim light. Louis could make out his face. It had angular features and he sported a long moustache. His face suggested he was around fifty years of age. He wore a panama hat that covered his hair, if he did in fact have any. Louis had noted a slight accent, perhaps Germanic undertones. Every so often a word would be delivered almost as a command. There was also a harsh rounding off to sentences that would suggest he was either German or East European.

However, most revealing of all was a large scar across his jaw. Louis stared intently at it.

"I was lucky Dr Symes, Afrika Corps, nineteen forty two." He was aware that Louis was scrutinising the side of his face. "When you have been this close to death Doctor, you continue your life with a complete disregard of your own mortality."

"But all Scorpions die at some point and sometimes from a sting of their own kind. They are like the dragons of the desert and if you are a dragon, then you must accept that you will never have a happy ending. " Louis' response had been swift and to the point. He would have welcomed an opportunity to test just how immortal this man was, but for now, given the circumstances and the two guns still pointing at him, he just smiled.

"Very amusing Dr Symes, yes you are quite right, but I see no Saints on horseback here, do you Doctor?" They both were now grinning. Louis turned to Sarah and gave a knowing nod. At present it was the only way of relaxing her. He could sense her shaking slightly on her chair. He wanted her to know that everything was going to be okay. As unusual as it was for him to feel trapped like this, the fact that he was more concerned for Sarah rather than himself provided the additional incentive to not do anything rash. He could rely on his own abilities and reactions to provide closure upon this situation very quickly, but unfortunately he had no idea how Sarah would react. It was maybe too much of a risk. However, there was of course the very remote possibility that this man sitting in front of him may just yet be of assistance.

"Okay Dr Symes, I am sure that this is not your name, but for now I have no problem continuing to refer to you in this way. Equally my name is of course not The Scorpion, but for reasons of security and business I prefer to protect my true identity. It keeps the intelligence on me down to an absolute minimum. The fact that you know how I obtained my scar will undoubtedly mean that you know more about me than the entire network of Western intelligence organisations put together."

This was true, Louis and Sarah had used every possible source of intelligence to try and obtain background as to who or what The Scorpion was. Their attempts had been futile, between the French, American and British, nobody held anything on this man. He was new to the game, or at least that's how it appeared to them both.

The Scorpion continued. "Despite what you may think, I am an honourable man. If I enter into a transaction, you may be assured that I will always complete my end of the bargain. If however, for whatever reason you were to let me down, then it is highly likely that you would both die. I trust I am making myself clear?"

Louis nodded, he had no fear of the threat, but there seemed the slightest of chances that this man could lead them to the Rembrandts. It was nothing more than a gut feel, but it had served him well in the past, there should be no reason why this should be any different now.

Louis responded, "I can promise you this, we are as interested in ensuring we can purchase your paintings as perhaps you are in selling them. Our client has a burning passion for Rembrandt, he has himself a superb private collection of many great masters, but it is Rembrandt who he prizes the most." Louis turned to Sarah, he was on very thin ice and he knew it. His lack of understanding of the subject at hand, could result in any chance of them leaving the room alive evaporating at any moment.

"Yes, he has three Rembrandts already," Sarah at last felt calm enough and now also compelled to assist. "He now wants more, as we mentioned earlier, money really is no object, you must excuse the little joke of there being ten missing Rembrandts. It is unfortunately the Doctor's wry sense of humour, but if you are willing to provide us with a Rembrandt, then you can be assured that we will not let you down."

The Scorpion nodded his head in agreement. The actions of these two strangers had convinced him they were indeed after something. In his world there was never ever such a thing as an easy transaction and when had he ever met a potential buyer that had not aroused even the slightest suspicion? These two had travelled half way round the world to obtain some paintings, to believe they were genuine was too great a temptation.

"I will provide you with a Rembrandt. The cost will be one million US dollars. I will contact you in three weeks. Provide me with a telephone number and we will call when we are ready."

Louis looked at Sarah, they had not been prepared for this. They had no idea whether the figure requested was a fair price, but they had to remain calm. For now it was imperative that they provide a credible excuse as to why they didn't have a telephone number.

"Bayswater, London, four four three six" Sarah calmly provided the details of a telephone number, she stared directly at The Scorpion, her fear had now almost completely subsided. She began to sense they were going to not only survive, but like Louis, believed that this may not a dead end after all.

Louis turned and slowly nodded. He immediately realised what Sarah had done, she had given them her home telephone number. In the circumstance he admired her bravery, but he also knew that soon, not only would they have her number but also her address. He therefore hoped she had not become too attached to her home as from now any return visits would only be solely for the completion of the mission.

"Have you any idea how long you will take?" Sarah was with every second sensing her confidence growing, "I'm sure our client will want to know."

"As I said, three to four weeks." The Scorpion responded, "but please, my dear lady, don't be too pushy, these things take time to arrange." Louis was experienced enough to realise that the painting was probably already primed for sale, but it was going to take a great deal longer for The

Scorpion to ensure that they were who they had suggested they were.

"Our business here is now finished." With that final comment the man arose and walked back towards the shadows in the corner. The two men immediately followed and the third moved to the doorway from where they had entered. He picked up the small Chinese man and walked back into the room. He too disappeared into the darkness. Sarah and Louis heard a door close. In the available light it was not visible, but there was obviously another door leading out of the room, but at this stage following the men would probably be a fruitless exercise. They would easily be able to melt away into the bustling streets of Hong Kong. Anyway a date had been set for within a month, there was a lot of work to do, not least ensuring that Sarah Caitlin had never lived in Bayswater.

It took several days to return to London. Without Abel's assistance, travel arrangements always seemed to take a little longer. Notwithstanding this, as the plane came to a stop at the gate back at London Heathrow Airport, Louis could see out of the window a departmental car with Abel standing behind it, looking intently towards the plane as the steps were manoeuvred toward the rear exit.

"Welcome back, both of you, I hope you both had a jolly good time in Hong Kong, now please come along, into the car, we have people waiting for us."

Louis smiled. There was something undeniably reassuring about Abel Harrington. He sometimes believed, that if his place in Hell hadn't already been guaranteed that in some peculiar way Abel may have been his guardian angel.

The car departed the airport and sped easterly towards London. Typically for this time of the year it was raining in London, but the weather was the last thing on anybody's mind. Neither Sarah or Louis could say with any confidence that their trip to Hong Kong hadn't been a complete waste of time, but for the time being this is all they had, other than a hunch that The Scorpion was undoubtedly able to get his hands on Rembrandts. Whether they were his, or he was going to take delivery from another source, they had been unable to gauge from their exchange.

The car pulled into a car park at the rear of the imposing Ministerial building adjoined to the Admiralty across from Downing Street. Sarah and Louis followed Abel up the steps and in through the revolving doors. Abel displayed his security badge to the men at the desk. Sarah was well known to the men. Louis just kept walking, his endorsement was the people he was with. They climbed two flights of steps and walked along a typically long Whitehall style corridor to the room facing them at the very end. The sign on the door denoted that this was the Minister's office. Abel tapped gently on the door and all three entered.

Sitting in front of a large desk was Colonel Mallory and facing him was a grey haired man with a pinstripe suit. Not unexpectedly, they were both enjoying a drink.

"My dear boy, how the devil are you?" the Colonel held out his hand and shook Louis' hand vigorously. "Now, why don't the two of you sit down over there and tell us exactly what you've discovered."

Louis couldn't quite work out why they were here. He wasn't even sure which Ministry they were in. But nonetheless he felt at ease with the Colonel and started to recount all that had happened since they last met. When they had finished, the Colonel continued, nodding.

"Okay, well not quite what was expected but never mind. We didn't think it was going to be a walk in the park." From the appearance of the Colonel, Louis reckoned it had been a while since the Colonel had walked anywhere of a noticeable distance.

The Colonel continued. "The most important thing we can do now is ensure that we are ready when they call. Minister, may I have your permission to make the necessary arrangements?"

The Minister nodded, he was obviously aware of the mission, but had decided to just sit and listen. He appeared intently focussed on what was being relayed. His only comment in fact, was his agreement to the Colonel's request.

"Of course, you must do everything possible to ensure success Colonel."

"Okay, Louis, I've arranged for you and Sarah to go the place we first met. Sarah, it will provide us with the time we need to ensure all records linking you and the house are erased. I believe it will also allow you to prepare yourselves for the next part of your mission. I would suggest the pair of you indulge in some background reading on Rembrandt. A little knowledge can go a long way you know." With that, the Colonel began chuckling to himself and turned back towards the Minister. He leaned across the table and refilled the two glasses. Louis and Sarah taking direction from Abel, rose from their chairs and left the room.

The drive to Dorking took just over an hour and a half. They arrived as the day was losing the last remnants of light. Abel walked them to the door and with a hearty pat on Louis' back bode them both goodnight and returned to the car. Sarah, more familiar with the surroundings than Louis, strode through into the hallway and across to a cabinet on the other side of the room. She reached into the top drawer and pulled out two keys, passing one to Louis she smiled.

"Here you are then, getting to be a bit of a habit this Mr Blue. Maybe you would like to dine with me in say, a couple of hours?"

Louis just nodded. He was enjoying the time spent with Sarah. On the last visit to the house he had doubted the sense of Sarah being sent with him on such a potentially dangerous mission, but since those very first moments he had looked forward to every second he spent with her. He was beginning to wonder if she could possibly feel the same way. There had been several instances when certain comments and mutual momentary glances had allowed Louis to entertain such a positive perspective. Yet, equally there had also been the cold terse responses that had rendered any aspiration almost preposterous.

All afternoon the rain in Munich had poured ferociously. The thunder and lightning had abated by early evening, yet there seemed to be no letting up of the incessant rain. It had been a generally wet autumn and start to the winter, but the last few days had been particularly stormy. Most people were staying off the streets, preferring instead to use the public transport or their own cars to move around the city. Only those with a dire necessity walked the pavements and Strasses.

Inside the perimeter of the Englischer Garten a sole figure was jogging past the Monopteros Temple. The weather appeared to the runner to be almost an irrelevance, a strong body and physical endurance were paramount and a little drop of rain was hardly going to stop the daily ritual.

Karsten Reinman was an imposing figure, standing nearly two metres tall. He had a muscular build and it was obvious to those determined enough to be out in the rain this particular evening that this man was committed to his regime. His tracksuit was soaked, but the unpleasantness of the weather merely added to his own conviction. He was dedicated not only to his physique but also to his profession. He had served his master well over the years, carrying out tasks whenever and wherever asked. Life was satisfactory, he was fortunate to own his own spacious apartment near the Rathaus. This had been due in part to the payments received for carrying out his tasks in such an efficient manner. He had grown up in Munich. He knew and cared for the city too well to leave permanently. His orders would often see him leave for several weeks at a time, but he always looked forward to returning.

It was well into the evening by the time Reinman got back to his apartment. He placed the key in the lock to open the door. As he applied the gentlest of pressure, the door swung open without the usual push. He had visitors.

Reinman immediately pitied anyone who had unknowingly been stupid enough to rob him of his possessions. Their problems were about to multiply, particularly as it would appear they were still there. Unless there was a whole group of men attempting to rob him, Reinman felt extremely comfortable that the odds were stacked well and truly in his favour.

He moved stealthily down the corridor, stopping at every doorway to identify as to whether it was in that room the unsuspecting intruders were located. At the end of the hallway was his living room. This was the room that overlooked the square and it was the only room with the door still closed. He grabbed the door handle and slowly began to turn it.

"Please Karsten, do come in, you'll catch your death out there in the hallway. I noticed from the window you're soaking wet, come in here, it's a lot warmer and also I want to talk to you."

Reinman, realising that the element of surprise lay with the intruder and not himself, pushed open the living room door. Sitting in the only armchair in the room, facing towards the window overlooking the square a man turned and smiled. Reinman recognised him immediately.

"Mr Harrington, how are you?" Abel stood up and walked towards Reinman, "It's been a while."

"I'm very well my dear boy, very well indeed. I see you're keeping fit. That's important you know. Great strength and a sharp mind go a very long way." Abel's reply was a little condescending.

Reinman was extremely well educated. He had a gift for physics, he had studied at Harvard and obtained a Master's degree from Oxford. His passion though had been art, even as a small boy, cutting edge he believed this was a result of having been raised in Munich.

Munich had in many people's view been at the forefront of the nineteenth and twentieth century art movements. It was a city well associated with culture. The Goethe Institute after all was located there and during the nineteenth century the arts had flourished under the patronage of both Ludwig I and Ludwig II. At the beginning of the twentieth century Munich was seen to be at the of the new Expressionist movement. *Der Blaue Reiter* group had been formed in nineteen eleven by the celebrated artists Wassily Kandinsky and Franz Marc. They were believed to have provided a seminal influence in the development of much modern art, so Munich had undoubtedly during the century become a cultural hotbed for art and its development. Karsten Reinman was in turn very proud of this fact and that this was the place he came from.

"Have the British not found you out yet Mr Harrington?" Reinman asked. "They task you with ensuring that the enemies of their state are eliminated and right under their nose it is you who is the biggest threat to their security." Despite their association, Reinman was a fanatical Nationalist, he despised in his country those who were traitors. The East Germans he had a particular hatred for, they were first and foremost Communists and being German came a very poor second. Abel was British, but the lack of comprehension of how he had been able to turn his back on his own country was there all the same.

Abel's expression changed almost immediately. He scowled at the young German. "I am proud of being British, I have served my country far more than you could ever imagine. I have undertaken missions that whilst they may not have prevented the falling away of our Empire, have ensured it's decline was not so rapid. I hold secrets that if in the public domain could see many governments collapse. Do not question my loyalty young man. You have no right to do so."

"But you are here are you not and we both know why you have come." Reinman's tone was now a little less confrontational. He realised that perhaps his comment may have been a little off the mark. Perhaps it was possible to serve two masters, as long as their paths did not cross. Then maybe one's sense of duty and loyalty could remain intact.

Abel's response was again delivered with an avowed assertiveness. "My purpose for being here and what I do, is done with a clear conscience. In every situation and every circumstance my loyalty and duty can never be brought into question. There are however times when, for the purpose of the greater good, we must take steps that not all will understand or agree with. I know my actions are inexcusable when seen from a particular direction, but for me, the alternative path of doing nothing is just as damning as the actions of any traitor."

"And no doubt the money helps?" Reinman's arrogance was by now pushing Abel's composure to its considerable limits. He prided himself however, on his ability at all times to maintain his composure. After all he had faced death himself many times and survived. In part, he put this down to having remained calm and steadfast when others would have crumpled.

"That of course is a welcome bonus." Abel smiled as he responded, looking around at the relatively comfortable but by no means grand interior of the apartment. This possible confrontation had been effectively diffused.

Both men sat down. It was obvious to Reinman that Abel was here for a particular reason. Being as it was extremely unusual for them to actually meet one to one. On the last two occasions, they had met with many others in attendance He looked at Abel, then duly beckoned him to deliver whatever he had come to say.

"My dear boy, you serve both your master and your beliefs well. We do all we can in our powers to follow what we know in our hearts to be right. Colleagues of mine have undertaken a mission on behalf of an ally to our country. It may yet have dire consequences. Considerable focus has been put upon this mission by key figures within our government. My belief is that if this assignment is allowed to continue unchecked, everything you believe in will be gone. If you, like me, wish to prevent this from happening then we must take immediate action to defend your master." Abel had always appreciated the drama of life. Any opportunity to regale with a tale which didn't always rely heavily on fact for emphasis, he did with gusto and in a manner that delivered to the listener a gripping perspective on sometimes the most mundane of facts. This time however, his comments needed no additional impetus. The enormity of what had been said left Reinman's expression almost lifeless.

"I will do what I need to. You know I will lay down my life if necessary." Reinman's response was hardly unexpected. Over the preceding several days much thought and discussion had gone into who would be the ideal candidate. It was the unwavering commitment of Karsten Reinman that had convinced others he was the right man. Under no circumstance could he fail.

Over the next hour the two men discussed the contents of Abel's dossier. It highlighted the activities of the previous fortnight, providing full background on the mission to The Caribbean. It had been his idea that Morientes should be set up as the primary suspect for the missing masterpieces. Abel was convinced that this would ultimately bring Louis back to square one. To the best of his knowledge Morientes had been nothing more than a drug baron who had a passion for art. As long as Louis and Sarah were unable to trace any hoard of missing masterpieces then in time the mission would simply be registered '*Incomplete*'. Any future attempts to focus resources on a wild goose chase would be deemed internally as unnecessary and everything would be returned to normal.

Whilst not admitting it to the German, Abel had been taken aback by the discovery of The Scorpion. Although this was still a considerable distance from the awareness and the subsequent discussions surrounding the purchase of Rembrandts. Abel was at pains to ensure the truth remained hidden. Both Louis and Sarah were ultimately on a trail that may in time bring them a little to close for comfort. It was imperative that they continued to be supplied with leads that would ultimately lead to a growing frustration with the mission. However, as concerned as Abel was, there were elements of his role that quite simply prevented him from going to far without compromising his own position. It had also occurred to him, that should they get too close to the truth, then there would only be one available course of action. Abel felt distinctly uncomfortable with this outcome. This reason alone would have been enough to guarantee that if such circumstances arose, it should be somebody else, not him that should carry that particular task. In Reinman he had a willing collaborator.

By the time the full details of the mission had been relayed to Reinman, he too appreciated the *gravitas* of the situation.

Whilst there would appear to be little chance of the full truth being discovered, he, like Abel did not believe it was a chance worth taking.

"I will do exactly as you suggest Mr Harrington. I will pack my things tonight and depart for London immediately. You have provided me with all that I need. Tell me Mr Harrington, is the Master aware of what I am doing?"

Abel took no discomfort from having to lie. He had been in Munich for the last twenty four hours, but he had informed no one. To an extent this was his mess, should he tell anyone of the people he was defending this would more than likely result in repercussions upon himself. When Marco van Rijn had requested that the Department help him recover his family's missing masterpieces, Abel considered that certain measures should be taken to ensure that if the need arose, everybody would be made immediately aware of the danger. But he had decided against it. Anyhow, at this stage he regarded the threat as almost an irrelevance and as such, it may actually be possible that The Master need never be informed. However, It always paid to have an active anticipation of what may happen in the future. Abel therefore ensured at least in his own mind, he had a 'disaster plan' that could be engaged at the first sign of any notable threat. He was all to aware that Lucifer Blue had not been blessed with a genius mind but equally, he had never failed a mission before, this fact alone made him dangerous.

"Listen Karsten, you must not fail this task, everything is riding on you. However, should you at anytime believe you are under suspicion or have been spotted, you must leave the country immediately. I shall give you this telephone number, but you must call only in the most extreme emergency. Under no circumstances, if you are found out, must you provide any information. As it stands, no one is looking for you or expecting you so you have the advantage. So don't lose it. If you are caught and you lead them to me then you are automatically endangering the Master, do you understand?"

It was now Reinman's turn to scowl. "You should know me better than that Mr Harrington."

Abel nodded, smiled and shook the German's hand. He left the apartment. The rain was still falling in the streets outside, but Abel's mind was too pre-occupied to notice. His secret had remained hidden for many years. There were very few who knew what he was so at pains to defend and he was unwavering in his resolute belief that it should also continue this way. He perceived it ironic that the hunter was about to become the hunted. He had no desire to see Louis harmed, but the resultant factors of his success would be catastrophic, of that he was convinced.

The sound of the rain pattering against the window woke Louis. He opened the curtains and peered outside. Autumn was now well behind them and the onset of Winter had begun. Many of the trees had since shed their leaves. However there were still a few evergreens dotted around the immediate garden grounds, providing a natural barrier to the land behind the house that stretched for a considerable distance. It would be at least another couple of hours before he would be offered breakfast so he decided to go for a walk.

Sarah's room was across the landing. Louis turned the handle on the door and slowly made his way towards the main stairs.

"Where are you going Louis?" Sarah emerged from the doorway. There was a faint light coming from her room, she looked as though she had been awake for hours.

"I thought I might go for a stroll before breakfast." Louis responded. He was not given to normally going for walks, but then much of what was presently happening in his life could hardly be described as typical. There was an increasing sincerity in his approach towards Sarah. The thought of the walk had been driven in part by the fact that this would give him the opportunity to both get out of the room and also consider what he was now feeling for Sarah. It was all completely new, a set of emotions he was certainly unaccustomed to.

"Do you mind If I join you?" Sarah's request was almost immediate, "I've been up most of the night going through the files on Rembrandt and the others. I really hadn't quite appreciated there was so much to learn."

Louis smiled, "I don't mind at all, in fact it will be a pleasure."

"Great," Sarah replied, "let me get my coat on and I'll meet you by the back door in five minutes."

The weather was still somewhat blustery, but the rain earlier in the morning had now passed and the sun was attempting to break through the clouds. They walked slowly down into the valley behind the house, passed over a little bridge that crossed a small stream and then continued to the forest of pines at the top of the slope.

The trees were packed quite tightly together. As a result the dead pines on the ground were still relatively dry. Louis sat down, placing himself against one of the larger trees.

"You look at home here Louis," Sarah remarked as she too sat down. "It's almost as if the more isolated and alone you are the more comfortable you appear."

Louis couldn't deny the accuracy of her statement. He had never felt relaxed around other people, notably ones that were still alive. He had always been a loner, but Louis was certain that nobody wants to grow old alone. In his more thoughtful moments, when considering retirement from his chosen profession, he would generally consider the termination of employment. Immediately this would lead him to almost assume that this date and the final moments of his own life would be exacted with a high degree of synchronicity. Yet every now and again he would imagine a partner, somebody to spend time with and care for. But he had always discarded these ideas as foolish thinking and extremely unlikely to ever happen. That was until now.

"I can't deny that Sarah," Louis replied, "I have always been alone, but please don't think that this is what I have always wanted. It seems appropriate that we should have this conversation here and now. My life has always seemed to have been spent in the woods on my own. As a child, I remember the forest as the only place I felt at home. It was in a place like this that I spent most of my formative years and it's there that I feel I have remained all my life. In fact, I've always been sitting alone, waiting at my tree, hoping that one day that right person may come along, someone to lie down beside me on the ground and watch the summer sun's rays dance through the branches. But till now it has always been winter in my woods, I sit alone, just me and the trees. Tell me though, if you ever found yourself walking where I sat, would you ever join me?" Louis looked straight into her eyes as he asked the question.

"I'm here now am I not?" Sarah reached forward and held Louis' hand. He gently pulled her towards him and she lay her head on his chest. Louis stroked her hair and looked out through the trees. He could never remember such intimacy as this. He wished they could stay here all day, but they had work to do that morning. He closed his eyes and wrapped his arms around her shoulders, gently kissing the top of her head.

Sarah slowly lifted her head as she whispered, "Louis, do you think you will ever leave this job?" Sarah's eyes focussed into the distance, yet it appeared that not only her eyes, but now also her thoughts were also beginning to wander.

"Actually, I was just thinking the very same thing." Louis' softly delivered response, despite nobody being close by, suggested that the intimacy of the moment was being enjoyed just as much by him, as it was Sarah.

"I have never really considered this is a job you can just walk away from," Louis continued. "But maybe if we can successfully complete our mission, then perhaps they may allow me to leave. But I would need a reason to move on." Louis took a lungful of air as he finished talking, the nervous anticipation aside, he didn't want the sound of his own breathing to muffle Sarah's response.

The reply however was not forthcoming. Yet Louis wasn't to be disappointed. Sarah instead sat up and kissed him on his lips. Her hand slowly stroked the side of his face. Louis could feel his heart race, the adrenalin pumping through his veins. He was unfamiliar with this sense of affection, but nevertheless he liked it very much. Many times he had faced death, remaining resolute and calm instead of the expected fear that would bring many men to their knees. Instead it seemed to simply pass Louis by. Ironic then, that one fleeting moment of tenderness should result in him responding this way.

"Come on," he said, carefully lifting both he and Sarah to their feet, " I'm famished." They walked slowly back towards the house. Louis kept his arm around Sarah's shoulders until they crossed the small bridge. It did not seem appropriate to allow others to see them this way.

Following breakfast both Louis and Sarah spent the remainder of the morning with their heads in their art books. It was a significant ask, but they had to convince professionals in several weeks time they were who they said they were. It was imperative that since they had stated in Hong Kong that they had a passion for art and that they were purchasing the paintings on behalf of an individual who himself was an art collector. Of course, it would also be entirely expected, that should any conversation arise on the subject pertaining to the transaction, they would be at liberty to discuss just about anything to do with Rembrandt.

Lunchtime approached, breakfast had been taken late but Louis, perhaps thinking subconsciously of Abel had decided to request some tea. He walked through the main hall towards the corridor leading down to the kitchen. As he passed the main door, he heard a tapping on the window he had just passed. Turning back, he rubbed away some of the condensation. It was Jonah Betts. He had disappeared when the plane had touched down in Norfolk.

Louis walked to the door, opened it and took a step outside into the cold. "Hello Jonah, what brings you here?"

"I need to talk to you Louis." Jonah's response had an air of urgency about it.

"Of course, come in."

"No, I can't, I need you to come outside, I have something very important to tell you." Louis hesitated for a moment, he sensed a somewhat disturbing undertone to the conversation. Jonah in turn, kept looking around the surroundings. His actions were odd, it was as though being spotted would almost certainly result in something sinister occurring.

"Okay Jonah, give me a minute to grab my coat. I'll meet you back over there by the stables." Louis pointed into the distance. The stables were approximately a quarter of a mile away in the general direction of the main gate.

Louis walked up the stairs to his room, he wondered what on earth could have so spooked Jonah. He knew very little of the man except he was trustworthy and not the sort of person to panic. There had been times over the past few years, when Jonah had managed to assist Louis in a tidy departure from some hell hole or another. Louis had accepted without question the bravery of Jonah. The past few minutes had therefore taken him by complete surprise.

Five minutes later, Louis entered through the stable's door. There was hay strewn across the floor, but the horses had obviously been moved to somewhere warmer for the winter months. There was a smaller stable to the back of the building and as since was no sign of Jonah from where he was standing, Louis deduced he must be there.

"Jonah, are you in there?" Louis whispered, the air of mystery had firmly grasped him. Even with the slightest suggestion of danger Louis automatically reverted to work mode. He lowered his body position as he neared the entrance to the second stable and felt for the knife strapped to his leg.

"I'm here Louis," the response from Jonah equally quiet.

"Okay Jonah, would you like to tell me what on earth is going on, you're acting a little out of character if you don't mind me saying."

"Louis, this mission you're on, I've reason to believe that all is not as it seems." Jonah sighed, as though the mission had already failed.

"What are you talking about Jonah?" Louis was now starting to lose a little patience. If there was a particular problem then it alarmed him that he had not already been told by any of the others. He was not in the mood for any dramatic build up. "If there if something I should know, tell me immediately."

"Louis, I'm sorry I have nothing specific to tell you. However, over the last few months I have become aware of strange occurrences. I'm talking specifically about the outcome of some high profile missions." Jonah was now beginning to relax a little, as a result his words were becoming a little more audible.

"Go on Jonah, continue." Louis was becoming increasingly intrigued.

"There have been times this year when we have placed our colleagues in the field. They were provided on the face of it, with what we would both consider some straightforward missions. The outcome though has been all to often a failure, it was as though they were expected."

"Are you suggesting there is a leak within the department?" If Louis had struggled to show any interest to this point, this had very quickly been forgotten. The thought that his life could be put in danger by someone who was supposed to be on his side made him almost explode with rage.

"I have no idea Louis, I really don't." Jonah took a look out of the stable window towards the big house. "There's someone coming."

"Okay, don't panic, it's only Sarah Caitlin, I told her I was meeting you here." Louis had decided to tell her after having picked up his coat. "You can trust her as much as you can trust me."

"Sorry Louis, I'm afraid I can't, but before I go you should know this, your departmental file has gone missing. There is information contained within which could put your life in considerable danger. It's imperative we meet again very soon."

Louis was a somewhat concerned at Jonah's lack of trust in both his endorsement of Sarah but more specifically what has just been inferred by the missing file.

"Jonah, how shall I contact you?"

"Don't worry Louis, I won't be very far away." Jonah leapt through the window opening at the back of the stable. Louis turned to meet Sarah.

"Louis, are you in there?" Sarah waited anxiously at the door to the stables.

"Yes I'm here, don't worry," Louis responded, emerging from the dark recess of the unlit larger stable. "Oddest thing, Jonah asked me to meet him and then didn't turn up. He probably just wanted to join us on our mission, maybe a little jealous of my new partner." They both smiled and walked back along the main driveway towards the house. But Louis' smile was merely cosmetic, Jonah's comments had gravely concerned him, danger and watching one's back in his line of work went with the territory, but it was usually the enemy you were concerned with, not some one who was on your side. From this point on Louis realised that even here in relative safety he would need to be constantly alert, after all, apart from Jonah Betts was there anyone he could trust? He turned and looked at Sarah, as unlikely as it seemed, from this point on, until he found out who the mole was, he would be wary of everybody

At a little after four o'clock in the afternoon, both Sarah and Louis were downstairs in one of the drawing rooms when they heard a car come across the gravel driveway in front of their window. Sarah, looking to take a short break from her reading, walked to the window and looked to the right towards the main entrance.

"It's Abel, he's coming in and there's someone with him." She turned towards Louis. "I don't recognise him," she then paused for a moment, "but he does appear quite handsome."

Louis moved uncomfortably in the chair and didn't dare look up, the reddened cheeks would immediately betray the twisting feeling he had in his gut on hearing this comment.

Sarah smiled and gave a little giggle, she knew she was teasing him, as she walked towards the door, she gently let her hand traipse over his shoulder. Again without looking up, Louis held her hand and gave it a gentle squeeze, Sarah went to open the door. He had been reassured.

Abel marched into the drawing room in his usual forthright manner. "Louis, how are you old chap, how's the revision going?" he asked.

"As well as can be expected I guess, not too many distractions thankfully." he glanced at Sarah.

"Good, that's fabulous, now I'd like to introduce you to somebody. This is Klaus Dieter Schmidt, he is an expert on European art and will be invaluable to our mission. Mr Schmidt has been brought up to speed with the mission to date. His task is to help you with any questions you may have on the forthcoming meeting with The Scorpion."

Reinman, comfortable with the alias Abel had provided him took a few steps towards Louis and held out his hand. "It is a pleasure to meet you Mr Blue."

"Please call me Louis." There was a slightly perplexed look on Louis' face as he responded. His thoughts immediately turned to the reason they were here, back at the house. "Well, may I ask why we are having to do all this studying, I'm a firm believer in being ready, but this is a little over the top is it not?"

"My dear chap, I just thought that you needed all the help you could get. Mr Schmidt will not in any way try and take over your mission. He merely is here to facilitate you, but of course I think it prudent he accompanies you both at all times when you depart."

Louis was furious, he had certainly no need for any assistance. His reaction had suggested that both he and Sarah were doing fine on their own. In reality, they were struggling and he knew it. He just didn't like the admiring look he was giving Sarah.

"Listen Louis, may I have a private word with you? It won't take long." Abel put his arm round Louis' shoulder as he asked the question.

"Of course Abel, let's take a step outside. It's awfully warm in the house, I could do with a bit of air." Louis was not accustomed to so many individuals needing to have a private word with him. This was now twice in one day, but if the meeting earlier on was anything to go by, private words appeared to have their uses.

"I'm afraid I've got some bad news." Abel whispered. He looked down and kicked some gravel across the driveway. Louis steadied himself, awaiting the coup de grace.

"We've been aware for a few months of a spy in our camp. Confidential information appeared to be seeping out to the other side at an alarming rate. We had our suspicions, but it was your coming back to Britain that finally nailed the culprit." Abel nodded as he spoke. He believed he had Louis' trust and he would therefore believe every word.

Louis just shook his head and sighed. "Abel, please tell me you haven't used me as some elaborate bait."

"No old boy, of course not. It's just your arrival here that kick started a chain of events. This in turn led to us finding out who the culprit was." Abel frowned as he spoke, as though offended by Louis' suggestion.

"Well who was it? Anybody I know?" Louis didn't so much ask as demanded.

"It was Jonah Betts I'm afraid." Abel shook his head, hoping to enforce the point that this discovery had also been a significant shock to him.

"Jonah, are you sure?" Louis was now totally bewildered. It didn't make sense. If Jonah Betts had been sent to do him harm, why warn him that his life maybe in danger.

"I'm afraid so," Abel responded, "I had my doubts about him all along. There were elements of his lifestyle that, how shall I say, were a little worrying. The need for money would have appeared to have recently taken on a growing importance in his life."

"So has he been taken in for questioning?" Louis asked, hoping he would himself be given the opportunity to ask a few questions.

"Actually no, he was found this afternoon, only a short way from here actually. Thankfully he had decided to take his own life. I can only think that in the end the treachery got the better of him and he ended it before he caused any more damage. We found him hanging from a tree."

Louis had not appreciated it till now, but that this may been the reason why Jonah had been so nervous. If it had been his intention to kill him earlier on, but at the same time he had been undergoing a moral crisis, then a lot could be explained. The refusal to enter the house when prompted and the frustration he demonstrated when learning that Sarah had been told of the meeting must have convinced him to wait for a more opportune moment to do his bidding.

"Abel, may I ask why I was the target?" Louis was trying to fit the last few pieces of the puzzle together.

"Simply put old boy, you are a complete and utter thorn in the side of some of this country's greatest foes. With you out of the way, the balance of power in our little 'underworld' would be substantially weighted in their favour." Louis looked quizzically towards Abel. The compliments were coming thick and fast, but that he was regarded as such an asset, a well known prized trophy should the other side ever succeed in killing him, left him in no doubt that he actually preferred the anonymity without the compliments.

"As a result they would pay an arm and a leg to see you out of the way Louis, so we can all thank our lucky stars Jonah was unable to complete his mission."

Louis was satisfied he had been told everything. Jonah's demeanour had been explained by his obvious ethical dilemma. With the mole gone, Louis could now focus again on the immediate task at hand.

Abel patted Louis on the back as they re-entered the house. Thankfully Louis turned the heavy handle on the door. Abel would have found it an almost impossible task. His hands were still stinging from the rope burns. Reinman had been unable to carry out the execution alone so it had been left to Abel to hold the rope as Jonah struggled his last vestiges of life. He hated himself for having to witness and take part in such a horrific act, but he just kept repeating over in his mind, that behind this mess lay a nobler cause.

For the next few days the primary topic of conversation was the great artists. But instead of developing a passion for art, Louis had found himself becoming more and more distant from the subject. Reinman had no such problem, albeit irrelevant. This was after all his first love. His passion for the paintings shone though in every discussion they had. Sarah had at times appeared to be charmed by his enthusiasm for them. She had also done little to hide her attraction to him when giggling at some of his well rehearsed humour. As a result, Louis had become a little distant. He had become aware of a whole host of new emotions over the past few weeks and now jealousy was being added to the list. He felt uneasy with Reinman from the outset, but now with his obvious flirtations towards Sarah, there was no doubting that Louis was developing in his own eyes a rational hatred of the German.

The attempts by the department to bolster the files on The Scorpion were unsuccessful. In fact it would be more accurate to suggest that the attempts by the department to provide any meaningful file was totally ineffectual. The only information they had was the first hand detail they had obtained in the initial meeting in Hong Kong. Unfortunately, they were going to have to do this one blind. This was unprecedented protocol, but then these were also exceptional circumstances.

Louis' frustration with the mission was beginning to show. He had been disturbed by the department's inability to point them in the right direction from the outset. In all the years he had served, his mission details had always been provided to him in a meticulous way. The target, location and timings were always exact. The outcome was of course always down to him, but he'd never known them to get it wrong like this despite the best endeavours of Jonah Betts. He had always worked alone, but as it was, not only did he have one additional person to be concerned with, he now had two and it was the second one who has fuelling his consternation.

The following evening there was a knock on Louis' door as he was readying himself for dinner.

It was Sarah.

"Louis, Abel and Klaus Dieter were wondering if we would like to pop out to the local pub for a drink this evening. They thought it may break the monotony of being cooped up here. I've already agreed to go. Please come it will be fun."

"Thanks," Louis replied, "I'll just stay here tonight, I actually wasn't really very hungry and truth be told I could actually do with an early night. You go and have a great time. Please pass on my apologies to Abel and tell him perhaps another time."

For the first time in the last several days, Louis spotted what he had been looking for. Sarah looked genuinely upset that he wasn't coming. Her head lowered as she turned and walked away from his room and down the stairs. Louis went to sleep that evening a little more relaxed than he had been over the previous few nights.

On Sunday evening, Louis had just finished dinner and was climbing the main stairs when he heard a car pull up at the front door. It was Abel in one of the department's cars. He turned and went to greet him.

"Okay Louis, get your things old boy, we're off. I'll just get the other two." Abel continued through into the main part of the house to collect Sarah and Reinman. Within fifteen minutes, they were all heading back into London.

Bayswater had a somewhat Bohemian charm. It had definitely fallen into line with other parts of 'swinging London'. For the last four years Sarah had enjoyed living there. It was only a few miles to work and the trip to and from the office on a London bus would entail much of the journey being along the Embankment, running parallel to the Thames. She would always attempt to sit riverside on the bus and watch the small dredgers and leisure craft drift up and down the river. There was less urgency on the river, with everything appearing to be done in a timely manner. Sarah would find this part of her commute almost therapeutic, particularly if it had been a tiring day, as this had recently become the norm, she had actually come to enjoy the ride.

Her apartment was not particularly grand but it did reflect in some small part the fashion of the day. The furniture was very in keeping with the late sixties, modern and cosmetic rather than cosy, but in truth, the reality was that her home reflected the dedication to her place of work. There was very little that suggested the owner spent much time at home. In fact there was a sparseness to the place that for anyone visiting would not suggest a warm welcome. It was obviously much more a convenience than anything else; a place to sleep and maybe not much more.

As the four entered the building Abel was busy informing the others of what to do over the next few days. He made it quite clear how imperative it was for either Louis or Sarah to be in the house at all times should the phone ring. Reinman could not stay. If as was expected the building would be watched in the days leading up to the call, a minimum of visitors would be required. In reality Abel and Reinman they did not care whether they were seen or not. In fact should the whole cover be blown, their task would be completed and the sooner everything would be returned to normal.

Over the next few days, the tension of the situation provided a different perspective on the relationship between the two. There was the occasional compliment and flirtation but Sarah's mind was more than preoccupied with the imminent phone call. She had never been as scared as when the knife has been held to her head in Hong Kong. Whilst she had managed to retain some of her composure, she prayed that she would never have to go through an episode like that ever again.

By the ninth day, apart from the short walks in nearby Hyde Park, both were beginning to feel the strain from the conditions they were facing. There had been very little to do in the apartment from day one. Any home designed merely for sleeping and very little else was not the ideal location to be holed up for any period of time. If anything it was a little easier for Louis. He had really only the boredom with which to contend. For Sarah however, when Louis took his mid afternoon stroll around the park, she would feel genuine fear. Any noise or neighbour walking up and down the stairs outside her door would lead to a substantial sense of panic. She would walk to the window and look desperately for Louis to turn the corner at the end of the street. Sarah knew Louis would never leave the building if he knew how scared she was, but she also knew how important it was for him to have a break from being cooped up all day, even if only for half an hour.

On this particular morning, both were at home. At just after eleven, there was a knock at the door. Sarah never had visitors, so it was highly likely it would be Abel calling to see if everything was ok. Up until now he had phoned on the dot at eight in the evening every couple of days, just to catch up and ask if anything was needed. Sarah went to the door. Despite her feelings for Louis she looked forward to there being someone else to have a face to face conversation with. As the door opened, she had expected to be met by Abel's cheery greeting. It wasn't until the door was fully opened and the light from her apartment lit the dark hallway that she saw the two men standing in front of her. Sarah had never seen either of them before.

"Hello Miss Ventner. We are here to ask you to come with us. You are interested in a painting are you not?" The man at the front who had asked the question was a large imposing individual and seemingly English. The other, a smaller man was oriental, Sarah immediately assumed Chinese.

Attempting to disguise her panic as she spoke, she replied, "I'll just get Dr Symes. He is here too." Sarah slowly closed the door without shutting it. She turned and walked to the living room where Louis was sitting reading a paper.

"Who is it, Abel?" asked Louis.

"No, it's them. They're at the door and they want us to go with them, Louis I'm a little scared."

"You have absolutely nothing to worry about, I'm here. Our men will be outside watching the house. They will have seen them come in. Grab a bag, I'll phone Abel and tell him we're off and to ensure our guys follow us."

Louis and Sarah followed the two men to the car waiting outside. It was a large Bentley, a nineteen sixty four Silver Cloud. Wherever they were going, the journey was going to be infinitely more comfortable than when travelling around in one of the departmental cars.

"Where are we going?" Louis enquired as the car appeared to be heading out towards the west of London.

The two men ignored the question, in fact for the next two hours, nothing was said by either man. Louis noticed a sign that indicated they were only forty miles from Bristol. At the next crossroads the car turned right. They followed that particular road for a few miles until they entered on initial appearances what appeared to be a small village. The road sign read 'Kemble' and underneath 'The County of Wiltshire'. The car continued through the village, carrying on for approximately another mile and a half. They came to a stop at a set of large wrought iron gates situated to their left. One of the men got out and pushed the gates open. They then followed the winding gravel drive down to a large Tudor manor house.

As the driver brought the car to a stop outside the main door, the other man got out and opened both back doors. Louis and Sarah climbed out and stretched their legs. Despite the relative comfort of the Bentley, it had been a long journey.

"Welcome, welcome." Louis and Sarah turned towards the main door. They immediately recognised the voice and then the scarred face. "How are you both? I trust you didn't mind me having you brought here in person, it's just I do actually prefer to meet face to face. I find telephoning so impersonal and you never know who's listening." The Scorpion smiled, fixing his eyes on Louis. "Now please do come in. You have of course been followed. That alas was to be expected, but lets not all stand outside catching a cold. Let us get inside and discuss what needs to be discussed, then you and your people can get what they want and I can get what I want."

Louis was pleasantly surprised and also somewhat assured by the reference to them being followed. It was very unlikely that these people knew who had actually followed them, but given the monies involved, whilst it didn't suggest for one moment utmost trust, it nevertheless didn't seem an imprudent action on their part.

"Now have you been able to make the necessary arrangements for the money Dr Symes?"

Louis sensed that this was going to be a short meeting. Their host had got straight to the point.

"Yes of course we have." Louis' response was almost indignant. There had never been any thought given to the fact that they would in time need to get hold of any money. There was no desire to do any transaction. They were merely required to find out as much information about the source of the Rembrandt and then take it. Money quite simply, didn't enter the equation.

"But first you must tell me Scorpion, as we are paying an awful lot of money for this painting, it is imperative you tell me where you got it from. The last thing my client would wish for is Interpol paying him a visit without knowing from where it had been sourced."

"I'm afraid that is impossible. That was not what we discussed." The Scorpion looked a little irate as he continued. "I will however tell you that you have nothing to worry about. There will be absolutely no one looking for the painting we have sourced for you. There will been no crime committed and as such you can expect no visits from any authority. I have seen the painting myself and it is a beautiful piece of art. Your client will be very happy with the purchase, of that you can be assured."

"I understand," Louis replied, "I'm just struggling to see how a Rembrandt can be genuine and not stolen. You yourself laughed when I referred to missing Rembrandts."

The Scorpion grinned as he remembered the comment. "Yes Doctor, but that is because you said there were ten. Only a fool would think such a thing. Now we have the painting for you, I assume you wish to continue?"

Louis nodded. He looked at Sarah and gave her a reassuring smile. The fact that the painting hadn't actually been stolen of late suggested that the source of the masterpiece was perhaps from an otherwise unknown collection.

The Scorpion opened a file placed at the edge of a table by the window. "In here are the details of the painting you are acquiring Doctor. It is presently waiting for you in Paris. I believed it unnecessary to transport it all over Europe as that would have meant taking pointless risks with customs."

Sarah had made a mental note. They had been provided with a clue quite substantial in the last comment, wherever the painting was coming from, they knew that it had originally been in Europe.

The Scorpion continued, "I have arranged for the painting to be in a small gallery in St Germain des Prés next Friday morning, the seventeenth. The gallery is situated in Rue Saint Benoit, close to the junction with Boulevard St-Germain. You will be met by a man. His name is Henri. You will ask him what year Rembrandt died and he will reply that he has never died since his work is eternal. You will provide us with a bankers draft for one million dollars.

We shall then exchange and go our separate ways. Do you understand fully what is required of you?"

Louis nodded. He replied in a confident tone. "Yes, we understand. You must however appreciate that whilst we are an agent for our client, our knowledge of art is a little restricted to only Rembrandt's we have seen. If you are providing us with an otherwise unknown masterpiece, our ability to confirm its legitimacy will be limited. We will therefore have a colleague with us. His name is Karl Dieter Schmidt. He is an art expert and art historian, I assume that will be okay?"

The Scorpion nodded, there appeared nothing unusual in the request. It would be irrational for anyone to part with this sum of money without complete conviction that they were getting what they believed they were paying for. "That will be acceptable."

Sarah was still feeling uncomfortable. The men were standing either side of her and whilst she couldn't see anything she felt sure that all of them were carrying guns. "Is that everything then?" she asked, trying to sound as relaxed and as confident as she could given the circumstances.

"Yes," the Scorpion responded. "I will have my men drop you just outside a town I believe is called Reading. The people who followed you will no doubt be outside somewhere. They will be able to take you the rest of the way. No point my men having to drive all the way back to London."

It was obvious to Louis that this would merely give The Scorpion enough time to clear the house and be on his way, should anybody decide to come looking for him. With this in mind Louis turned towards him and commented rather than asked. "This isn't your house."

"Of course not," came the reply. "I have merely borrowed it from the owner. They will return on Monday and will never have known anything unusual occurred whilst they were away. I told you before Doctor, It is very important to me that my true identity remains hidden."

The two men shook hands. Louis and Sarah spent the entire journey back to the drop off point in silence, going over in their minds all that had been said. They were struggling to grasp any connection with ten missing Rembrandts. However, at this stage there was not a lot else to go on and at the very least the department could very soon have a new painting, albeit expensive, to adorn one of their meeting rooms.

As predicted, Louis and Sarah waited no longer than five minutes before a department car picked them up. Inside other than the department's driver were Abel and Reinman. They had followed them all the way. Should anything have gone wrong Louis would have expected back-up to be close by. Unbeknown to them both however was the reality that Abel was eager to ensure that should they have picked up any meaningful information, both Abel and Reinman would endeavour to make certain nothing could come of it. Abel hoped that this would merely involve subversion of the information they had attained, but he was all to aware that if necessary, Reinman would be invited to carry out the ultimate preventative course of action.

"Well what did you find out? What did they say?" Abel asked with an usual eagerness to his questioning.

"They have a Rembrandt for us," Louis replied, "It's in Paris. They have given us an address, a coded greeting and a demand for a banker's draft for the sum of one million dollars."

"Is that it?" Abel felt a little more relaxed upon hearing that very limited information had been gauged.

"There was something," Sarah replied. "The Scorpion made a reference to the transporting of the painting. It appears wherever the painting has come from, it has not been stolen and is therefore from a private collection. Secondly it has come from inside Europe and more than likely not France."

"Well that's something at least." Abel tried desperately to sound enthused, but despite the information being relatively harmless, it was nevertheless a step closer to the truth. He felt decidedly uncomfortable. Abel looked back to Reinman who sat motionless in the back seat beside Louis and Sarah. His eyes moved slowly towards Abel and he gently shook his head, a reassuring gesture to ensure Abel remained relaxed. At present there was nothing to cause undue concern.

The car took them straight to the Ministry. As before, Colonel Mallory was with the Minister. The information gathered at the meeting was delivered almost word for word. With the Minister's agreement, a banker's draft was to be prepared for the payment of the painting. Louis was a little taken aback at the ease with which the request had been agreed. Marco van Rijn was obviously held in the highest regard, all the way to the very top. It wasn't until they were about to leave that the Minister spoke in earnest.

"You will of course ensure the money is returned at some point won't you Mallory. This money belongs to the taxpayer."

"Do not be concerned Minister. Of course we will. I will personally ensure that the money is returned safe and sound." Mallory's response could not have possibly been any more insincere. To him, Marco van Rijn has been an extremely useful ally in fighting first the Nazis and now the Communists. It was obviously his belief that risking a mere one million dollars was the least the Dutchman deserved.

On the Thursday evening Sarah and Louis set sail from Dover. They were not alone however, Reinman had been instructed to join them. He was the art expert after all and would be required to authenticate the painting. It had been decided that taking the ferry and then continuing the journey from the coast to Paris by car was the most prudent form of travel. The flights from London to Paris were few enough to almost guarantee that as soon as they arrived at the airport they would be most likely followed. The sailings were thankfully more numerous and departed from more than one port. It was highly unlikely they would be spotted.

After a few hours sleep in a basic hotel on the outskirts of Paris, the three caught the train into the centre. Arriving at Gare du Nord they picked up a taxi. The weather was wet and windy, but a little like London, Louis believed that Paris actually impressed more in the Winter. There was something significantly appealing about large European capitals with the backdrop of the large impressive buildings set against a grey sky. He had been in Vienna the previous winter. Like his knowledge of art, his expertise in architecture was equally limited, but he had not failed to be impressed by the majesty of the buildings in the heart of the City. For several hours he'd actually taken it upon himself to do some sightseeing. He had spent the afternoon appreciating mankind's creativity, only for several hours later to be standing alone above his victim. It was then mankind's ability for destruction in this particular instance, that only he had been privileged to acclaim.

No more than five minutes later, having crossed the Seine they were outside the gallery. Louis paid the driver and the three entered through the unlocked wooden door. The room inside was well lit but not particularly large. In the corner by a door leading to a back room was an antique desk and a chair. On the wall were paintings of what appeared to be Parisian landmarks and all the work of the same artist. As they had entered through the main door an bell attached to the wall had rung, thereby notifying the proprietor that someone had entered the gallery.

"Bonjour Mademoiselle, Messieurs." From the room at the back a diminutive man approached them. He was about sixty years of age, grey haired and dressed in the apparel typical of an artist. His top was covered in paint and in his hand he carried what appeared to be well-used artist's brush.

"Bonjour," Louis responded. "We were wondering, do you know what year Rembrandt died?"

"Monsieur, Rembrandt will never die, his works are eternal. Please follow me, my name is Henri."

The three moved forward into the backroom. The room appeared dark as they approached through the door, but upon entering, it opened up and looking to the left they could see that there was a very large skylight allowing the whole area to be bathed in bright light. There was an easel with a painting depicting a river scene.

"Monet" Reinman remarked, noticing Louis studying the painting.

"You know your artists Monsieur," Henri commented, "It is a little pastime of mine. I do copies for certain clients. It pays very well."

"I'm sure it does," Reinman responded. He despised those who produced forgeries. There were many people who had unknowingly purchased what they believed to be masterpieces. Three years earlier he had read of an elderly couple in America who had paid a small fortune for a Klimt, only for an expert to later identify it as an imitation.

Louis cut in, he could see that Reinman was more than a little agitated by the artist's pastime. My name is Dr Symes. This is Miss Ventner and this is Herr Schmidt. If it is okay with you we would like to see the painting."

"Of course, if you will just give me one minute." With that the man walked to the middle of the room. He lifted a trap-door and descended into a basement, returning a few moments later with an object under his arm covered in cloth. He crossed to the bright side of the room where the others had remained. He lay the object down on a table and proceeded to unfolded the cloth. Inside, within an innocuous frame was a painting of an old man sitting at a table with a candle burning on it, he had his head in hands.

"Remarkable," Reinman was taken aback. He had expected to see a Rembrandt and knew there were others in existence, but this was his passion and he could therefore not prevent himself from being in awe of the painting in front of him. The others found chairs and sat down, but he remained standing, spending the next fifteen minutes closely examining the work. In the interest of his own mission, whether the painting was real or not should actually have been an irrelevance, but as he continued to investigate the authenticity, he was becoming convinced and in turn thrilled by the fact that the painting was indeed a Rembrandt.

"All I can say is that I would be astounded if this is not an original. It has the same tones and texture as The Supper at Emmaus, that was painted in sixteen twenty nine. It is my thinking that this was done at around the same time. It is beautiful." Reinman was truly astounded by the simple canvas. He had been somewhat surprised by his own reaction. He just looked, unable to avert his gaze. He understood the motive behind the sale. But if possible, he would have done anything in his power to return the painting to where it had come from, but he knew this was not his business.

"Are you sure Schmidt?" Louis asked. The mission had been challenging enough, but the last thing he now needed was to have to go on the trail of a Rembrandt forgery.

"Without a doubt," Reinman responded, his reply had been slightly delayed. He was still getting used to his alias. The affirmation had been delivered with such certainty however that Louis was assured they had a Rembrandt.

"Right Henri, we will take the painting and here is your banker's draft. The small Frenchman took the document, he walked over to a small safe, placed it inside and locked it by turning the numbered dials. At that very moment, two men appeared from the conservatory at the back of the house. They were familiar, they had been the two men that had come to Sarah's apartment in London. Reinman had been a willing recruit, successfully serving the cause on many occasions. However, other than Abel and several other men who would from time to time require him to undertake assignments, Reinman neither knew, nor was aware of anyone else's identity within his group of 'followers'. These men were quite possibly his colleagues. But since Abel had decided to not share details of Louis' mission with anyone other than himself, Reinman appreciated the need at this stage to maintain his false identity. He therefore moved himself as inconspicuously as he could behind Louis, keeping his gaze fixed firmly to the floor

"Unfortunately," Henri began to speak as the two man approached, both carrying guns, "the draft will take several days to enter our account. It is of course an extremely prudent way of payment, but it is not without its risks. Therefore we have no choice but to hold on to you for several days, as a form of guarantee. Miss Symes, please come with us."

"No," Louis' immediate response highlighted his concern. His voice almost shook. "Take me, I'm just as good a guarantee. Please let her go." He could see the terror etched across Sarah's face. He had expressed reservations all along about her accompanying him on the mission, but he had craved her company so much, that now his failure to have done the right thing had led Sarah directly into danger.

Louis considered attacking the two armed men, but he had two colleagues to protect. He had no idea how they would react. It was also very possible that somewhere in the room Henri had a gun hidden, so for now his only option was to do as they asked.

"Okay, good, now please Mademoiselle, please follow us." Henri pointed in the direction of the conservatory. One of the men had his gun pressed into Sarah's lower back. She began to walk forward rather tentatively. She turned to Louis as she passed him. Louis could see the fear in her eyes.

"Don't worry, I'll be with you very soon. Trust me." He had tried to assure her, but he could see how traumatic all this was for her, he cursed himself that he had allowed this to happen.

Behind the conservatory, there was an old brick wall, in the middle of the wall was a small door. It was through this that the three men and their captive departed. As the door closed, Louis turned to Reinman. "Come on let's go, we have no time to waste." Where they were to go and who they had to see Louis was himself unsure, but he was confident that staying where they were would not hasten Sarah's return.

The following day Louis was back in London. He had made contact with Abel and both had agreed that as no means of communication had been discussed when Sarah was kidnapped he should return to her flat. They assumed that was the only way The Scorpion knew how to contact them.

Louis kept trying to reassure himself that all would be fine. After all, he had merely to wait for the money to be transferred into The Scorpion's bank account and then Sarah would be released. He promised himself that as soon as she was back he would tell her exactly how he felt. He sensed a twinge of excitement that within several days she would be safe and aware of his feelings. He went over it in his mind time and time again. How perfect everything could be if she was to reciprocate how he felt.

But Louis was no optimist, he knew exactly what he was capable of doing and that which he was not. He left nothing to luck and believed wholeheartedly in the principle of actively anticipating the worst. By preparing for that particular scenario, Louis believed this would always provide him with the advantage of never being caught unawares. Once the money had been received by The Scorpion, what guarantee was there that Sarah would be allowed to live? After all, it was more than likely that she already knew too much.

Within moments, the mood of exhilaration he imagined would be forthcoming from the imminent reunion slowly began to change. Louis' thoughts were now truly focussing on what he now believed was the likely event of Sarah being tortured to death. He imagined her screaming, calling his name, trapped in some hovel desperately trying to escape. The rage grew within him. He hated himself and all those who had put her in this position. If only he had convinced her of the perils ahead, she would be safe now. But the truth was that he had enjoyed her company to the point that irrespective of the dangers, he wanted Sarah by his side. As much as he tried to ignore it, the basic fact was that if he had been more insistent, she would have remained out of harm's way.

As ever, Louis began to envisage what he would do when confronted, as inevitably he would be sometime soon, by Sarah's captors. The adrenalin began to pump through his body. He was more than capable of wanton destruction when calm, however, the devastation he was capable of if this rage continued to fester would be frenzied. He sat down in the chair by the window. Louis appreciated more than anyone that imagining revenge and allowing himself to become embroiled in negative emotions would only hinder the chances of ever seeing Sarah alive again. For her sake, he would need to stay mindful of the job at hand. He had been provided with a mission and he had no reason to believe at this stage he would fail. If in the meantime he could rescue Sarah along the way, then all the better. There would be a time to set her free, of that he was in no doubt. For the time being though he had other things to consider.

It was about five o'clock in the evening on the third day following his return from Paris, when there was a knock at the door. Louis could feel his heart pounding faster, he almost ran to the door, his craving for it to be Sarah completely engulfing him. To his disappointment it was Abel and Reinman.

"Hello Louis. Anything?" Abel was trying his hardest to sound jovial, but he knew how Sarah's predicament was affecting him.

"No, nothing at all," Louis responded in a dejected manner. He too had hoped that Abel might actually have some information for him. "I can't believe we led her into this Abel. It's all our fault."

"I know Louis, I feel terrible about it myself, I keep going over and over in my head how we could have played this very differently." As Abel continued, his head began to lower and his voice quietened, "I have something to say that I don't think you are going to like I'm afraid. The banker's draft, it was a forgery. It's worthless."

"Christ, have you any idea what we've done Abel? We've just signed her death warrant." Louis was almost frantic with despair. "The very second the banker's draft is discovered to be of no value it will assume about the same level of importance as her life. We've killed her Abel."

Abel for once was stunned. He felt desperately ashamed. He had never wished for any of this to happen. He had a fondness for Sarah. He had known her for many years, since she had first joined the department. Apart from her beauty he had always admired her dedication to her job, but now he had played a significant part in putting her life in terrible danger.

"Abel," Louis was anxious to find how this had happened. "When we were with Mallory and the Minister they were acting as though the draft was real." Why did we use a forgery?"

"The Colonel felt at the last moment that the risk was too great. Officially we have no use for the painting. All we care about is where it came from. There was in all honestly little expectation on the part of Mallory that the acquisition would lead us to the missing Rembrandt's. He believed that if we were going to find anything out, then it would have been at the transaction. From that point on the willingness to part with that much money was seen as excessive, so the draft forgery was provided." Abel's reply had been delivered with the sadness it was obvious Louis shared.

Reinman had been sitting by the window the whole time. He had been surprised to see Abel react this way. Sarah was after all just a pretty English girl who had wanted to go on an adventure that had backfired. Yet he watched Abel very closely. It was imperative that he remembered the importance of Louis' mission being a failure. They both served his Master and whilst the impending death of Sarah was unfortunate, they would be able to report back very soon that their own mission had been a complete success. He was still oblivious to the fact that apart from Abel and himself, there was no-one, including the Master, who was aware of the unfolding events

"Come on Abel. Let us go." Reinman stood as he nodded towards the door. "There's very little we can do here."

"No, I can't do it. I must tell him." Abel's response had been delivered with almost a rage in his voice. "I cannot be responsible for Sarah's death. We must do everything in our power to save her. Louis, I've something to tell you."

"Yes Abel, What is it?" Louis looked puzzled.

"I've been preventing you from succeeding in your mission. I made sure that you and Sarah were sent off on wild goose chases, but unfortunately you came a little too close with your trip to Hong Kong. I knew I was putting you both in danger, but I did nothing to stop it. That man standing there, his real name is not Schmidt. I brought him in to assist me should you get to close. Louis I'm so sorry. It was also me that assisted in the murder of Jonah Betts." Abel lowered his head. The shame was evident. For the first time since they had met Louis saw Abel's façade alter immeasurably. He looked a broken man, as though the enormity of his actions had in one brief moment delivered a crushing blow upon his conscience.

Reinman turned towards Abel. He was unable to hide his absolute hatred of what Abel had just done. He had once regarded him a disgrace to his country, but had excused him as his betrayal to his country was due to a greater cause, but now, he had done the inexcusable, he had wavered when he was required to be most resolute. It would be obvious to Louis that not only Abel but Reinman had also been guided by an ulterior motive. Reinman put his hand into his pocket and pulled out a pistol. It was a Luger. For years it had not been the weapon of choice for most, but Reinman was both a classicist and a nationalist with a strong sense of history. He pointed the gun directly at Louis. As it stood, he was of course the greater danger.

"Sit down Louis. This won't take a moment," Reinman's tone was calm. The immediate anger following Abel's comments had now passed. He knew he had to act quickly. His actions would therefore need to be instant and direct.

Louis had very little choice. He was too far from Reinman to exact any notable form of attack. The Luger was old, but even so, Louis realised he would be dead before he managed to get within striking distance of the German. He therefore calmly sat down and sighed, smiling at the almost sterile onset of his impending death. He had imagined that when he died, it would most be likely in the final stages of some glorious gun battle, or maybe some carefully timed explosion, but to die in this manner was not what he had expected at all.

Reinman lifted his arm to take aim. Louis closed his eyes and as he did so, he heard Abel yell and leap upon Reinman. The struggle lasted less than several seconds, just long enough for Reinman to fire one shot. The brawl ceased almost immediately. Abel sank to his knees and then fell to one side. Reinman froze for a moment, Abel's actions had left him stunned and now he had just killed him. The momentary lapse was what Louis had been waiting for. He sprang to his feet as though a coiled spring. His hand had dropped to his ankle, his knife with the serrated edge was withdrawn from its sheath and immediately thrust into Reinman's throat. The Luger discharged another bullet, but the direction of the shot was into the floor. Reinman struggled but it was all in vain, Louis withdrew his blade, the edge of the knife tearing at the vital arteries as the knife re-entered, but this time it was into his heart. Louis would rarely feel any emotion when watching the last moments of someone's life ebb away, but Abel was now dead and Sarah had more than likely been murdered by her captors. He nodded his head and gave an almost arrogant smile as Reinman's eyes slowly closed and he fell to the floor.

There was an eerie stillness in the room that contradicted sharply with what had just taken place. Two bodies lay on the floor. Louis himself had stopped. He remained still as he considered the events of the last few moments. Major obstacles to him completing his mission had been removed, but what remained of his mission? Who could he trust and where could he go?

He walked to the window and gazed outside. The winter sun was beginning to disappear over the horizon. Louis felt an emptiness that had become all to familiar over the previous years. The feeling would always be that much greater as he left the scene of a completed mission. As the target lay motionless on the floor, it was at that moment that Louis felt most devoid of humanity and as outcast from society as anyone can be.

"Louis old boy." Louis turned round. Abel was still alive. He fell to floor beside Abel's curled body.

"Hang on Abel, I'll get some help." Louis was desperate to keep his old associate alive.

"No Louis," Abel gargled, the blood was teaming from the side of his mouth. Louis had seen this many times before. There would only be a few moments left.

"Louis, I'm so very very sorry," after every word, Abel took several seconds before he could summon the energy to deliver the next one. "My dear friend, you must rescue Sarah."

Louis almost fell backwards, Sarah was still alive. "Where is she Abel?" Abel slowly turned his head to Louis, his eyes beginning to close. "Abel, for Christ's sake, where is she?"

"Munich, near the Rathaus, Schmidt's real name, Karsten Reinman, he has an apartment." With that last vestige of life Abel's head fell to one side. He was dead. Louis rested his hand on Abel's shoulder. He had given him hope that Sarah was still alive and if alive she would be probably be somewhere in Germany.

He hadn't a moment to lose. Louis grabbed the little he had with him and left for the Ministry. He knew that there he would get some time with Colonel Mallory. Any feelings of revenge that he may have felt following the forgery of the banker's draft had now been replaced by a burning desire to rescue Sarah. He would need the Colonel's help and there were really no other alternatives. He left the building and boarded the first bus he saw heading in an easterly direction with Westminster listed as one of the destinations on the front. Within forty five minutes he was sitting in front of both the Colonel and the Minister. They were as intrigued as they were shocked by the details of the days unfolding events.

As Louis was finishing his explanation of recent events, or to be more precise, how he could simply not comprehend why Abel had taken his course of action the door opened. In walked Marco van Rijn.

"Good evening gentlemen. It's good to see you all again." In keeping with his elegant appearance van Rijn had a certain grace in the way he greeted people. He shook all three men's hands enthusiastically. "Now please tell me exactly where we are. Do you know the location of my paintings?"

"I'm afraid not quite yet," Colonel Mallory replied. "I do believe however that we may be closer to the truth than we think." Louis was slightly taken aback by the Colonel's choice of terminology. 'The truth' suggested there were circumstances Louis was unaware of, maybe even lies, but he decided against asking the question directly. It would perhaps be prudent to just observe and listen. The Colonel poured himself a drink, sat down and began to describe what had happened during the day and to explain why Sarah was missing.

"Okay that's good, at last we're getting somewhere." The Dutchman's response re-ignited the rage within Louis surrounding Sarah's abduction.

"You bloody fool van Rijn. What about Sarah?" Louis barked. "I cannot believe you think we're getting somewhere when Sarah is either dead or perilously close to it. Can you not think of anything else other than your damn paintings?"

"Louis, of course you are right. I wasn't thinking. It's just that its been twenty five years of searching, waiting and hoping and now I feel I am so close I sometimes lose my sense of perspective. Louis, I know what it is like to love someone with all your heart, only to then lose them. I am sure that Sarah is alive and where we find my paintings we shall find Sarah."

Louis was calmed by the apology. There was indeed sincerity in the words and sorrow in the Dutchman's eyes as he recalled the loss of his wife. Louis was a little puzzled however by the reference to him loving Sarah, he had no intention for it to be so obvious. He realised that Abel's periodic updates had probably made reference to the growing bond between the two of them. His most recent outburst had probably confirmed the fact, should anyone have been in any doubt.

Nevertheless Louis felt the need to respond. "Love? What's that got to do with it Marco? Sarah is innocent in all of this, she was merely doing her job trying to help you, I can't help but feel we have let her down. Trust me, it's not love that has annoyed me, it's that we and that includes you have a moral duty to get her back."

"Of course Louis," the Colonel responded saving van Rijn the need to reply. The Dutchman had been broken by his reflection on his own feelings and any further comment would be unnecessary. Louis had made his point, van Rijn's posture confirmed Louis' comments were not lost on him. Getting Sarah back alive had a growing number dedicated to the cause.

"Okay gentlemen, enough has been said for now." The Minister had been listening intently to everything being discussed, perhaps unusually for a politician he preferred to communicate his suggestions and instructions only once he had fully understood the circumstances. "Louis, obviously you must go to Reinman's apartment, search it and should you draw a blank, wait there. We can only hope that whoever these people are they will try to contact Reinman sooner rather than later. Marco, I'll leave it up to you, either you can accompany Louis or you can wait for us to pass on any development."

"I think I'll go with Louis." The response from van Rijn had not been what Louis had hoped, but having got used to partners on the mission over the last few weeks he had no serious objection to this suggestion.

"Okay gentlemen," the Colonel's enthusiastic tone immediately brought a sense of focus back to the mission. "You shall leave in the morning. We'll arrange flights and all the usual back up. Good luck and we'll see you very soon with both the paintings and a certain young lady," the Colonel winked at Louis. He smiled. His earlier protestation that he was not in love in Sarah had obviously been futile, but so it should. It had been a lie after all.

Munich was covered in a blanket of thick cloud as the plane descended towards the airport. The death of Reinman would require Louis to be even more alert than usual. Both he and van Rijn had decided to have minimal contact. It was more than likely that whoever they were hoping to find would know them by their appearance. The Scorpion had Sarah and he would of course expect them to look for her. But it would be unlikely that he should have any reason to believe they would ever actually find her.

Louis was beginning to feel somewhat tired. Until now the mission itself had not been unusually stressful in terms of effort, but the emotional element had taken its toll. Losing

Abel and possibly Sarah had put a quite considerable pressure upon Louis. He desperately wanted to find Sarah, but perhaps now, just as important was the answer as to why Abel had done the unimaginable. They had not been what most would consider friends, but Abel was as close to a kinship Louis could ever remember having. As a result, he continued to question over and over in his mind Abel's actions. They had undoubtedly taken Louis by surprise. But as the period of time since the momentous event in Sarah's flat grew, so did Louis' awareness of the fact that there were still significant aspects of this affair that left many matters unresolved. Now in Germany, his single hope was that these issues were about to become an awful lot clearer. Abel was dead. There was no bringing him back and therefore no means of obtaining an explanation, but somewhere or someone would provide an explanation as to why he had betrayed not only his colleagues but also his country.

The taxi, pulled up outside Reinman's apartment. The Ministry had very little difficulty in obtaining his address from public records. Even if the information had not been forthcoming through the public directories, the Ministry had enough contacts within the German departments of security to ensure that it would only be a matter of minutes before everything would be known about Karsten

Reinman. As it was they had checked as a matter of course, yet the files on Reinman provided no insight into why he should be involved. His qualifications highlighted his preferences for the arts, but other than this rather tenuous link, there seemed little else.

The entrance to the hallway was open. Both men ascended the staircase. Louis put his hand in his breast pocket, picking locks such as this was easy. He had been trained to open safes with the most minimal of accessories, so these sort of hurdles could be overcome in a mere couple of seconds. By the time he had pulled out a small leather wallet the door was open. It would appear that van Rijn's exploits since the war had also included illegal entry.

They entered the apartment and immediately began to search for any clues, correspondence or any other form of information that could help them understand the man a little better and who or what he had ultimately been protecting.

The rooms were generally sparse. There were no immediately obvious pieces of evidence that provided any pointers. There were no letters, no files providing instructions, just books, lots of books. In fact in nearly every room there appeared to be books, stacked in no particular fashion.

After several minutes perusing the piles in front of them both van Rijn picked one of the books up and inspected the cover closely.

"Have you noticed anything odd about these books Louis?" van Rijn asked.

"No, nothing." Louis looked puzzled. They were all seemingly in German, so it would be unlikely that he would be able to offer any creditable link between the various titles.

"If I'm not mistaken Louis, all these books seem to have some form of reference to the war and the Nazis. I wonder if our dead German was in fact a Nazi sympathiser?"

Louis immediately remembered the unusual choice of weapon in the Luger, but the evidence was still a little flimsy. The war was still in most people's recent memory. It had been just over twenty years since the cessation of hostilities. Since then, Germany had gone through a period of substantial reconstruction. It was understandable that many young academics would have a morbid curiosity as to how and why the circumstances and events leading to the war had come about. However, both men agreed. For the subject matter of all the books to be the Nazi party was indeed a little odd.

"Marco, come through here. I think I may have found something." Louis had walked through to the kitchen. On one of the walls there were several photographs stuck to a board. They all seemed to be of Reinman in various art galleries. Beside the photographs was a calendar. It appeared that it had been as a substantial reference file, red and blank ink denoted all the major appointments and journeys undertaken. Crossing out most of the month was a simple entry, it read 'England'. Either Reinman was stupid in providing such insights or perhaps he was simply forgetful, or maybe he was just so confident that he would succeed in his mission that there was no danger anyone would see this information.

It was not the calendar alone that had caused Louis to call for van Rijn. Beside the calendar were a couple of vouchers, van Rijn immediately recognised them as rail tickets. They were not dated and so it could easily be inferred that they were not restricted to any particular period of travel. The fact that there were two suggested that Reinman would not be travelling alone, perhaps it had been intended that Abel would accompany him, Louis had thought. They had not been marked, other than on the back of one of them had been scribbled four numbers, one eight three five. Louis assumed that Reinman, appearing to be a forgetful man must have written his preferred time of departure. They had not been punctured either. It was therefore an obvious deduction they had not been used. The destination on the ticket was Kassel. A little like England, Louis had no significant geographical knowledge of Germany, but he was familiar with the name and knew immediately it was German. It would appear that Reinman had planned to make the trip soon after returning from England. It now seemed that the most obvious course of action for Louis and van Rijn would be to make use of the tickets, after all the original purchaser would have little use for them.

Louis made a short phone call to Colonel Mallory. He explained the finding of the rail tickets. Mallory agreed that whilst unsubstantiated for now, it was the only clue they had found, a trip to Kassel would be prudent in the circumstances.

By now it was late evening. Sarah's life still appeared to remain in the balance. For all Louis knew she may have been dead for days. That thought kept on ripping through him like nothing he had ever felt before. He struggled to keep his composure. On each occasion he imagined her dead, he could feel his heartbeat rise as the panic set in, yet time and time he checked himself. He knew he had to be calm, Sarah's life may depend on it.

The following evening the two men boarded the train for Kassel. The city lay about three hundred miles to the northwest of Munich. As ever Louis was impressed by the punctuality of the trains, the service and the picturesque landscape they passed along the way. Marco van Rijn had made it clear that he had no love for the Germans or Germany. He had experienced and witnessed some of the harsh horrors of war. It was still a vivid memory to some, but Louis guessed for those who witnessed it, an eternal scar would be left on their souls. The loss of van Rijn's wife, murdered by a German would never allow van Rijn to feel comfortable whilst in Germany. Louis deemed it therefore impolite to mention how attractive he believed the countryside to be and how the post-war reconstruction had been extraordinarily successful.

As they departed the station Louis began to feel his instincts kick in. The journey had provided a pleasant respite. The level of conversation between the two men had been kept to an absolute minimum, perhaps they were more alike than both men would care to admit. Yet now despite the picturesque town centre and smiling faces, Louis began to focus his attention on the task at hand.

For him it was Sarah. Across from him in the taxi sat van Rijn. He too was deep in thought, yet Louis imagined he was thinking only of what he would do with the paintings, should he ever find them.

Marco van Rijn had been an informal agent of the British for nearly a quarter of a century. Unlike Louis whose orders were very rarely anything other than the termination of an enemy of the nation, van Rijn's activities had called for greater subtleties. As a result he would often spend months at a time in a foreign country/ Over the years he had mastered many languages. The ease with which in this particular country he discussed a place to stay with the taxi driver demonstrated that despite his experiences German was no exception.

The two men booked into a charming hotel in the centre of the city, just off Wolfhager Straße. Other than the tickets, there was no significant reason why they should be here in Kassel. They arranged to meet in an hour in the lobby and to start searching, although both felt privately it was most probably going to be like looking for a needle in a haystack.

The centre of Kassel had many local shops, it seemed selling mostly food. Louis imagined for a moment he and Sarah sitting outside one of the small coffee shops, drinking and chatting without a care in the world, but it was only for a moment. Within seconds he felt his stomach tighten as he imagined her lying dead in some darkened room.

The men walked for several hours. They saw a great deal of Kassel, but nothing that gave them any sense of being closer to the paintings, or in Louis' case Sarah. They decided to stop and take some refreshment inside one of the many coffee houses.

"Louis this is ridiculous. We don't even know what we're looking for. We can't imagine for one moment that he will be here," van Rijn sighed as he spoke in an unusually dejected manner.

"He, you said he, who do you mean?" Louis asked, puzzled by van Rijn's reference.

After several seconds of thought that were not wholly convincing, van Rijn responded. "I mean Rembrandt of course. His paintings were an extension of his mind and soul, when I speak of the paintings I always refer to 'he'."

Louis nodded, the response had not totally convinced him, but he imagined it was plausible enough, even though slightly unusual. He had never heard a collection of paintings referred to as a pronoun of the painter. Nevertheless he was no expert on either the paintings or as to how they should be referred, so despite the last few weeks studies, he decided to let it go.

"Okay," Louis pepped up, trying to inject a sense of optimism into his associate. "We must think as though we are Reinman. Let us consider why he has come to Kassel and what he would do when he gets here. I received confirmation from the Colonel when I called him from the hotel there are no Reinman's listed in any Kassel directories. We can therefore safely assume he was not coming here for family reasons. It must be something to do with his visit to England. Whoever employs Reinman must have something to do with Kassel. Now what else have we got?"

Both men sat quietly looking at each other. It was evident that there was very little else to go on. There were no galleries of any significant size. There were two small art studios with retail outlets, but that was just local art, students trying to make money to pay for their expenses. The look of amazement from one of the artists when asked if there were any Rembrandts on display anywhere locally had convinced both men, if the paintings were in Kassel, they were most definitely not on public show. Equally, if they were here, the people of Kassel had no idea that such art treasures were close by.

The men finished their drinks and spent the rest of the day searching through the local library references, looking for recent local mentions of Rembrandt. They visited the Fridericianum Museum, but as it was not renowned for its art, they had little joy there. Marco van Rijn would occasionally ask people about the paintings in a very roundabout way, often making conversation about his love of art and in particular Rembrandt, but always to no avail.

At the end of the day both men were exhausted. They had crossed back and forth over the river on numerous occasions. Irrespective however of which side of the water they were on, their mission had been a spectacular failure. Louis suggested they should go back to their respective rooms, rest for a while and then eat downstairs in the hotel's welcoming dining room. His proposal was greeted with a nod of approval from van Rijn.

As Louis entered the restaurant he saw van Rijn was already seated. "Listen Marco, I'm not to sure if we're not perhaps wasting our time. We could spend days here looking for something and someone who may be hundreds of miles away. Abel had mentioned Munich after all. Perhaps a safer bet would be to return to Munich and see if another avenue develops. What do you think?"

"Reluctantly I have to agree with you Louis. There is nothing here that is obvious. Perhaps we were a little hasty coming here in the first place without any solid leads." Again van Rijn sounded dejected. It was apparent that he had a considerable expectation resting upon their trip to Kassel.

"Okay, let's do that. I've got the train timetable here. We'll go back in the morning." With that Louis opened the small information sheet.

"What is it?" van Rijn asked, surprised by the look of extreme curiosity on Louis' face.

"Marco, please pass me the train tickets." He duly did as he was asked.

"Look," Louis continued, "the numbers on the ticket, I presumed they were train times from Munich to Kassel, eighteen thirty five, but according to the timetable, there are no trains leaving Munich station at that time and," there was a slight pause, "there are no trains leaving Kassel at that time either."

Both men immediately realised that they may have just been provided with another clue. They becoming more and more convinced that the numbers must have a growing relevance. Perhaps a telephone number or maybe the security code for a safety deposit box somewhere, but as enthused as they were by the exciting discovery, both were aware it was late and the town had in essence closed for the night. They would continue their search in the morning with renewed vigour.

The church bells rang, breaking the silence of the early morning. It was now seven o'clock. Louis had arranged to meet van Rijn downstairs in the lobby.

"You know we could actually get someone to do this for us Marco," Louis grinned, van Rijn was not an early morning person but he felt inspired by Louis' comment. They had received a substantial clue last night and now it appeared Louis had an idea that would assist them further. Both men sat down in a couple of the chairs.

"Behind you Marco, that young lady, she's a receptionist. When I call London I go through her. If you ask her kindly,

I'm sure she will assist, I'm sure that should those numbers be a telephone number, then we'll have our answer."

The nodding smile from van Rijn signified not only his agreement, but also that in the next few minutes the challenge of finding what they were looking for could be overcome, far sooner than they had dared to hope.

"Wish me luck," van Rijn strolled across to the desk. Louis was unable to hear what was being said, but he saw a lot of smiling. He was not a young man anymore but van Rijn still had an abundance of charm and it was being displayed in significant quantities with the young receptionist. Less than two minutes later van Rijn returned. He nodded approvingly to Louis who was unsure as to whether this implied he had been successful in obtaining an address for the numbers or that van Rijn was just pleased with himself for still being able to impress young ladies with such ease.

"Well?" Louis asked. He rolled his eyes as van Rijn had chosen to sit down again without relaying what had been.

"Oh Louis, what would you do without me?" van Rijn smirked. He knew exactly the effect his silence on the matter was having on Louis.

"Come on you old dog, what have you found out?" Louis was a little amused by van Rijn's teasing but time was being wasted and they were far from completing their mission and that included finding Sarah Caitlin alive.

"Grundstücksmasler," Louis looked somewhat bemused by van Rijn's statement, "Estate agent," van Rijn continued, "they're no more than half a mile from here. We can be there in ten minutes."

Louis felt his spirit soar with the good news. The last few days had been intolerable not knowing whether Sarah was alive or not. The death of Abel Harrington had upset Louis. Despite his wrong doings, Abel had come good in the end, yet he knew that somehow there had to be a reason for Abel's actions. He was no traitor. the pieces were all there in front of him. At this stage however, he was simply just unable fit them all together.

By half past eight they were outside the estate agents. The name above the shop stated that the owner was a Herr Müller. The two men waited outside for several minutes.

They discussed a strategy, basically this was what to say. With Louis' very basic German the plan was made even simpler.

Louis and van Rijn entered the shop. A little bell rang as the door opened. A middle-aged man of approximately fifty five years old, grey hair and a tanned complexion stood up. He was tall, taller than both men by several inches. Despite his age he also looked incredibly fit. He wore a suit that suggested that business was very good, Louis guessed it was Italian.

"Guten Morgen, ich heiße Herr Müller, kann ich ihnen helfen?" The man greeted them both with a handshake.

"Guten Morgen,"van Rijn responded in perfect German. He then asked the man whether he spoke any English.

"Natürlich, several of my best clients are either British or American. Many decided to stay on in Germany after the war and my business has grown with no inconsiderable thanks to them." Louis moved towards the estate agent. What had threatened to be a very long confusing conversation would now be understood.

"My friend and I are looking for a property, something quite significant. We have a business that requires us from time to time to entertain on a grand scale. As a result we will require something slightly rural, but as I mentioned something with sizeable grounds and lots of space within the house. We will also need a well lit house but not to much direct sunlight." As van Rijn continued with his specification of the house they required, Louis felt that it was unlikely this was just being cobbled together on the spot. It was much more likely that he was in fact describing a house that he either now resided in or where he had once lived.

When van Rijn had finished, the estate agent nodded and walked to the back of the room. Louis and van Rijn glanced at each other. Louis raised his eyebrows and slowly shook his head. The conversation about the house was interesting but it did not appear to be helping them move any further ahead in terms of the mission.

"Tell me gentlemen, if you don't mind me asking, what is it you do?" Müller asked.

"We are involved with art and particularly great masterpieces. It is our passion and our life." The reply from van Rijn who by now had sat down almost knocked

Louis backwards off his chair. He had been becoming frustrated by the futility of the conversation regarding the house, but this last comment had gone straight in for the kill. It was a high risk strategy.

The estate agent's demeanour changed almost immediately. For a moment he looked at them with a puzzled expression. It was enough for both Louis and van Rijn to believe that this man likely knew of the paintings and for Louis it meant that he probably knew where Sarah was being held.

Louis considered the next course of action. The most prudent thing would be to continue the discussion. After all, many people have a love of art and keep many great collections. The estate agent could soon be putting the whole episode down to coincidence. The alternative would be to reach across the desk and threaten to beat him within an inch of his life if he was unlikely to otherwise provide them with the information they sought.

As it was, it was van Rijn who made the decision to keep talking. He concentrated upon their need of a house. "When I say we have a passion for art I really don't want to give you the wrong impression. Our collection is vast but very amateurish. We both have a love of painting and as all artists do, we like to display our works. As a result that is why we need the substantial areas, in order that we are able to display them. Our association with the masterpieces relates purely to reproductions. We have a thriving business involved in the retailing of prints."

Herr Müller appeared to relax, the comments had seemed to do the trick. He sat down and again began to discuss the two men's requirements. A confident grin covering his face, he believed that very soon he would be making another sale.

Ten minutes later the conversation concluded, it was agreed that they would return the following day to see some available properties. This would give the two men time to watch the shop and if necessary follow the estate agent. Both were in agreement that Müller was implicit in what was going on. The only question to consider at this stage was what did an estate agent have to do with a collection of missing Rembrandts?

Louis and van Rijn left the office, thanking Herr Müller for his time as they departed. In Louis' view the estate agent was guilty. Despite the fact that there was no significant incriminating evidence, he had a feeling. It was in his guts and over the years that had served him well.

The afternoon came with nothing of note having happened at the estate agent's office. Louis considered it very unlikely that anything would be gauged from sitting across the street, anyway he could only drink so much coffee.

"Marco, when he's gone, let's break in. If there's anything there linking him to The Scorpion the office is so small I'm sure we'll find it." Louis was becoming increasingly frustrated with sitting around waiting for developments. He was a man of action. There was a time to wait and there was time to act. His natural predilection was for the latter. It was this course he believed they should now be taking.

As van Rijn turned to Louis, considering his own reply, a large black car parked up alongside the office. Almost at once the door to the office opened and Herr Müller came out, turned and locked the door and then began walking towards the car. He had his case with him. It appeared he had finished for the day, but it was just a little after three o'clock.

"Finishing early," Louis' remark had no real sense of suggestion. It was merely an observation. That however was about to change. As the estate agent got closer to the car, the driver got out to open the door, Louis sprang forward in his seat. The driver was one of The Scorpion's henchmen. He had seen him first in Hong Kong and then again at the house in Wiltshire.

"That man, I recognise him. He's one of The Scorpion's men. Quick Marco, we have got to follow them." Louis jumped to his feet as beckoned van Rijn to follow. The traffic on the road was thankfully slow, with so many cars leaving and joining the main thoroughfare the black car's movement would be considerably hampered.

Thirty seconds later and Louis and van Rijn were in pursuit. Both men were at ease and extremely able when it came to stealing a car. The fact that it was Louis who broke the window of the old Mercedes, fiddled with the wires under the wheel and then began to make the engine roar was purely down to the fact he had sprinted in the direction of the first available car. His companion was there several seconds later and jumped into the passenger seat.

"Louis are you sure about the man?" van Rijn asked. "He was only out of the car for several seconds."

"Of course I'm bloody sure Marco. He was one of the men who threatened Sarah. Trust me, I would not forget that face."

The car accelerated. The traffic ahead was still moving very slowly, but Louis had decided that this was hardly the time to obey the rules of the road. They were still far enough behind the black car that the noise of the horns and yells from other drivers who they were edging indignantly aside did not attract the attention of the car up ahead. When they were within five cars of their prey they slowed down. The traffic ahead was easing. They would soon to be able to follow the car at a closer distance. Louis was well versed in tailing cars unnoticed. It was something he had been called upon to do on many missions.

Both cars left the town to the west. The landscape changed as soon they were in the country. With the cars on the road becoming more and more scarce, Louis felt obliged to drop back some distance. His partner, who's only sign of ageing was his deteriorating eyesight, squinted to keep his eyes on the car ahead.

After thirty minutes the car ahead began to slow. There was a turning to the right that seemed to lead to a winding road rising up a hill. The side of the hill was covered in thick forest pines. To follow them would be foolish. Louis realised that they had no idea where the turning lead. They could quite easily turn a corner and be met by an unwelcoming reception party. He decided to drive past the turning for a quarter of a mile before parking.

"Come on Marco, we will have to walk from here."

The Dutchman nodded. He was still extremely fit, yet even so the hill looked quite a challenge, but he realised that Louis was right, the option of continuing to use the car was to much of a risk.

Both men were armed. For Louis that was almost always the case. More often than not he would forget he was carrying a gun, but at times like this it was habitual. He would always put a hand down his side to check,. This time was no different. They had no real idea what they were walking into.

Rather than follow the road, the two men took a more direct route up the side of the slope. It afforded them more cover as the large pine trees were quite tightly packed. They could hear the noise of the woods echoing all around them. The occasional sound of a bird of prey calling as it swooped on its target provided a chilling atmosphere. The night was starting to close in and it was bitterly cold. The men reached the top of the slope and decided to lower their bodies down into a crouch else they be exposed as they crossed the highest point. The two of them were a little out of breath when Louis quickly gave a whispered command.

"Quick, get down," both men dropped on to their fronts and looked ahead, down into the small valley below them. They could now see that the road that had wound up the side of the slope they had just climbed snaked down the other side to what was a substantial looking Gothic castle. It appeared to be at least several hundred years old. If it were not for the severity of the circumstances, then the scene before them could almost have been considered enchanting, yet the atmosphere was providing a chilling backdrop. The castle was well lit and in most of the windows there appeared light coming from inside. It seemed beyond any doubt that it was inhabited.

In the courtyard there was an array of cars. The big black car carrying Herr Müller was just coming to a halt at the end of a row of similar looking vehicles. Two men, including the estate agent got out of the car and walked through what appeared to be the main door.

Louis looked around the outer perimeter of the castle. There were high walls circling the entire building, the only break being for what looked like a portcullis. On closer inspection, Louis soon realised that the place was being guarded. There appeared to be two sentries at a gate just short of the crossing into the castle and on the outer wall he could just make out in the fading light men walking along the top. There appeared to be about eight in all. The option of getting into the castle, if this was to be an option, at this stage was becoming increasingly perilous.

Below them on the slope the trees were providing similar cover to that on the side they had behind them. They would be able to crawl down the slope to the first sentries undetected. The light from the castle was still far enough away to ensure that the darkness of the night continued to afford them additional protection.

"Louis how are we going to get in?" van Rijn asked scanning the outer wall for any noticeable weakness in it's defensive layout. The castle had been built though at a time when the likelihood of an army encamped outside the walls looking to attack was a little more likely than today. It appeared that any attempt to breach the wall would be flawed on two fronts, the height of the outer wall and the patrolling sentries. What was clear to both men however was that whoever or whatever was inside the walls was well protected.

"Well we can't go over the wall Marco, that's for sure. However we get in, it'll have to be through the main entrance."

"Okay let's do it," van Rijn replied.

"Hold on Marco, we can't just go up to the sentry and ask nicely 'can I have a look around your very interesting castle.' We're going to have to wait a while. The only way we can get in will be car or van, anything else and we'll be dead before we get anywhere near the front gate."

"When I was your age, my men and I would have thought nothing of storming the front gate. We would be in through the front door before you knew it." van Rijn almost grimaced as he spoke, as though the opportunity for a heroic deed was about to be lost.

"Steady Marco, how many men would you have lost in doing so? In case it has escaped your attention there are only two of us against at least ten maybe more. Now in a darkened room or with the element of surprise I wouldn't generally have a problem with that, but an approach through that gateway will be suicidal." Louis was not one to shy away from any form of confrontation, but he knew which battles could be won and those that would be lost. His successful completion of assignments would normally require days waiting patiently for the right moment to strike.

The silence from van Rijn suggested in some small part an agreement with Louis' response. He didn't want to be seen to back down, but he realised it had been a foolish suggestion. Nonetheless Louis was impressed with his bravery, although he also realised that the comments had more than likely only been stated for nothing more than such a demonstration

Louis searched the immediate area. He had spent many nights in the cold, therefore he also knew the importance of trying to stay warm and the need to get some sleep. There was nothing the two men could do for now, but Louis hoped that maybe with the morning's sunrise they may get a better perspective of the challenge ahead of them.

The key in the lock turned slowly and the door opened. The creaking of the large door reverberated around the room, Sarah Caitlin quietly stirred. A man walked in and put some food and a glowing candle on the table in front of her, she was lying on a small single bed, she looked up.

"Where am I?" she asked. Her eyes were now beginning to get used to the dim light in the room. She immediately pulled the bed sheet up around her neck. There was an icy chill in the room.

"Eat!" the man's reply was brusque and to the point. He had no desire to enter into any conversation. As it was,

Sarah felt extremely tired. She guessed that as she had no recollection as to how she had got here then she must have been drugged. Her attempts to stand were very laboured. She felt a slight irritation in her arm and on closer inspection she could see where the needle had been inserted. Her assumption had been correct, but that didn't help her. Of more immediate concern however was where had she been taken and how long she had been there.

The man left the room, locking the door behind him as he went. The room was sparse with only a token light emitted from the candle. Sarah was not hungry. She was too busy taking stock. Her head still a little dizzy, she tried desperately to remember all the circumstances leading to this predicament. She sat back down, put her head in her hands, closed her eyes and quietly began to cry.

"Surely they must have received the money by now," she whispered to herself. There seemed little sense to her that if that was in fact the case that she should remain a captive. If the monies had been transferred as the draft requires, then what on earth, she thought to herself, was she doing locked in this room? After several puzzled moments however, a chilling thought crossed her mind. Could it have been possible that something had in fact gone wrong during the financial transaction? As much as she tried to quickly erase the thought from her mind, Sarah was now preoccupied with the terrifying consideration that she would soon be sacrificed as a means of revenge.

Sarah lay back down on the bed, her eyes focussed on the ceiling. She desperately hoped that Louis was looking for her. She knew he was capable of many things, but if she had no idea where she was, how would he?

For several hours she just stared blankly towards the ceiling. Every few minutes the tears would again run down her cheeks. Convinced these were her last few hours alive, she begin to think, as many people do in such a situation of all the things she wished she had done and of all the things she wished she had said. She had only known him for a short period of time, but several of these regrets were centred around Louis.

There was very little noise in the room to distract her, save the occasional footsteps outside the door and the subsequent creaking of the hinges when one of the guards put some food or water through the slat. She now considered escape, after all she had nothing to lose. She was going to die soon anyway, perhaps she could hide in the shadows behind the door. If she were to crouch down, when the guard next looked though the slat to check on her, alarmed at her disappearance he would enter the room. If she were able to find something large enough she could perhaps knock him unconscious and escape. But instead, she slowly sat back down on the bed. It seemed a pointless task. There was nothing to use as a weapon and where on earth could she go she thought to herself. Her only other option was to try and escape by attempting to remove some of the stones in the wall, but these walls appeared extremely thick. Their design had probably been based around avoiding that very possibility. The room reminded her of some old castle dungeon she had seen so many times in the films at the cinema. But this was for real and Sarah Caitlin was genuinely petrified.

As the flame from the candle appeared to be taking its last flickering leaps, she heard the footsteps again, except this time there seemed to be more than one set of footsteps emanating from the room outside. She could also hear voices. The key turned in the lock.

"Ah Miss Symes, you are awake, or should I call you Miss Caitlin? In the last few hours I have learnt a little more about you, I'm still somewhat unclear as to why you are here however, but I'm sure that will become apparent all in good time."

Sarah sat up and cowered back towards the wall. It was The Scorpion and as usual he was not alone. He was accompanied by several large men.

"What do you want with me?" Her terror was obvious in her tone. She tried to focus her thoughts on Louis and imagining him coming to rescue her. She was attempting to be brave but given the circumstances was finding it incredibly difficult.

"Your stupid paymasters have left you high and dry Sarah. That banker's draft was a forgery, worthless. However all is not lost, they have our painting but we have you." He laughed as he could again see the panic in Sarah's eyes.

"Did you really think we would have just passed over the painting without any form of security?" In the short time you have known me Miss Caitlin, do you really think I am the kind of man you could double-cross?"

Sarah shook her head. She had no real idea what kind of man The Scorpion was but she knew he was capable of murder, in turn she knew she was very scared and for now that was enough.

"You are right. Your attempt at betrayal was foolish, but sometimes we all have to learn lessons the hard way. Just think of it as merely one of those occasions." He was enjoying his moment. The Scorpion appeared to be taking more pleasure in Sarah's discomfort. She realised this and now almost as a means of rebellion she tried with every sinew in her body to stay calm and resolute.

She kept repeating Louis' name over and over again in her mind. But every time she looked up, there were the same men, all with their menacing expressions. She feared for her life, what was left of it.

"However Miss Caitlin, my master had decided you will live, for the time being anyway. He believes you to be worth more alive than dead. I don't particularly agree with him, but this is how it shall be." The Scorpion scowled as he inferred upon Sarah her good fortune. As a result, she began to feel a little easier knowing the 'Master' whoever he was had decided she should live. Although the temporary basis of this arrangement ensured she could feel not fully relax, she had been at least granted a short stay of execution. Perhaps there was still time.

"Does that mean I can go?" she asked. She raised her eyebrows and intently began to nod her head, as though inviting the men in the room to agree.

Almost at once all the men began to laugh. "Please Sarah, don't be so foolish. Until a mutual arrangement can be agreed with your employers, you will not be leaving here." The Scorpion grinned as he delivered his bad news.

Sarah's head slowly lowered till her chin almost touched her chest. She sighed as she started to gently shake her head. "This is so unfair. I did not ask for any of this." she tried not to be heard, but her whispers echoed around the room. The men turned and left the room one by one, locking the door firmly behind them as they went.

Again she was alone in the room. The light from the candle had now almost completely gone. She turned and faced the wall. She had been thinking for the last few hours only about the whereabouts of Louis, but now there was another thought beginning to cross her mind and that concerned the identity of The Scorpion's master. Whoever he was, perhaps despite protestations from others, he would have appeared to have done Sarah a considerable favour. Yet she fell short of bestowing too much favour upon him for showing such generosity. She was still a prisoner and there was no evident suggestion that this particular predicament would be imminently corrected.

It took Louis and van Rijn less than an hour to assemble shelter for the night ahead. They dug a small furrow near the base of some trees. They broke some branches as quietly as they possibly could to provide a layer for them to sleep on. They could also act as a form of cover with the larger branches placed up against the trunk of the tree. In the process this would provide much welcome protection for their dug-out. It was not large or all that comfortable, but it provided protection from the biting wind and would perhaps even more importantly provide a genuine camouflage should any sentries decide to patrol the slopes across from the castle entrance.

As it was both men were tired. The exertions of the last few days had taken their toll, especially for van Rijn. As soon as they lay down in their shelter, Louis, who had expected a little light conversation before they fell asleep was evidently the only one awake.

Thankfully both men managed to sleep for most of the night. They had individually been required to construct short term lairs on many occasions in the past. In van Rijn's case, it was from having to hide from pursuers. For Louis it was not unusual for him to sit and wait for the right moment to strike a target. His missions had taken him to many places when the luxury of a room had either not always been afforded to him or in turn not proved very useful when monitoring a target. So as temporary shelters in the forest go, this had been a roaring success. They were able to sleep for four hours and they had to their obvious relief, remained undetected. Given van Rijn's perpetual snoring Louis was amazed they had not been discovered. With a little light jibing, he let van Rijn know.

The two men moved again to a slight clearing that provided them a clearer view of the castle. It was now breaking daylight and the entirety of the castle, its size and the seemingly impossible task of breaching the defences were significantly clearer than they had been the previous evening.

"Get down, quick." Louis buried his face into the ground as he whispered an immediate warning to van Rijn. No more than 50 yards away, what appeared to be a small bus was winding its way round the apex of the hill and descending down the slope towards the castle. Louis slowly raised his head, looking in the direction of the bus. He could see even from this distance that the bus was full. The people sitting on the side Louis was able to see appeared to be all men, all wearing coats and most wearing hats. Whilst all men however, there was very little else he could distinguish from where he lay.

As the bus entered the courtyard to the castle, Louis' thoughts regarding the individuals on the bus were confirmed. One by one, men and only men disembarked. They were all carrying cases, whether containing papers or personal belongings Louis couldn't tell, but each one walked through the main door and into the castle. Louis counted eight.

The bus returned up the slope and down the other side. Again both men withdrew into the cover of the trees as the bus neared them and then moved forward again as the bus disappeared down the other side of the hill.

For the next hour or so, there was very little movement in or around the castle, apart from the odd sentry walking the walls, peering periodically over the top of the wall to the ground below. However, the silence of the early morning was again disturbed by the same bus. This time there appeared to be fewer people on board. Repeating the process of the first visit, the men entered the castle and the bus returned back up the slope. Over the next two hours, the bus returned three times. There appeared to be a break of about forty minutes between each return visit.

" I have an idea," Louis spoke with a degree of relief in his voice. The defences of the castle had been a little demoralising until now, but van Rijn could sense almost immediately from the look in Louis' eyes that he had a plan.

Louis grabbed a twig and began to mark lines on the ground. He ushered van Rijn to move in closer and began to inform him of his plan.

"We can the use the car. We'll position it by the entrance to the slip road. As the bus turns into the road, we'll hijack it. After several visits it is highly unlikely that the security will be looking for anything suspicious. On the last trip the sentry let them through without checking the bus." Louis continued with his diagram in the ground, but van Rijn needed no drawing. He fully understood what Louis had suggested and could himself not think of a better plan.

"What do we do with the people on board Louis?" The question was not so much a request for an answer but more of an affirmation as to a course of action. Whoever was on the bus was unlikely to be friendly. Who or what they represented was still unclear, but nonetheless given the perspective of the mission, they were expendable.

Louis just nodded. He didn't need to answer but notwithstanding that he felt inclined to respond. "Let's just hope there aren't too many people on board, for their sake."

The two men hurriedly returned to the car and drove back along the main road to the turning. They turned the car to face up the hill. Parking at the side of the winding road near the bottom of the slope, Louis sat in the car and van Rijn waited by the junction.

Ten minutes passed and van Rijn had not moved. He was hiding behind a tree, periodically looking round it, both left and right before pulling back. There was a constant flow of traffic, but there was no sign of a bus. Another twenty minutes passed, still nothing. The Dutchman shook his head and began walking the fifty yards up the slope to where Louis was waiting in the car. Louis could see van Rijn in his rear-view mirror. At the moment van Rijn was just about close enough to obscure Louis' view down the slope to the junction, the bus turned towards them off the main road. Louis frantically waved to van Rijn to get down. Luckily van Rijn was alerted almost immediately. He quickly moved to the side of the car furthest from the road taking full advantage of a high verge. He sat there crouched as Louis took off the hand brake. The car slowly ran backwards into the middle of the road, Louis then engaged the brake. It was imperative that the bus could not pass.

The bus came to a halt, stopping no more than several inches from the car, Louis in his wing mirror could make out the driver sitting at the wheel. He looked extremely irate at the obstruction and within several seconds was pushing the horn at regular intervals. With a continuing degree of impatience he then began to rev the engine of the bus, his intention being to imply that if action was not taken soon to move the obstruction, he would take it upon himself to undertake the manoeuvre forcibly using the bus to move the car out of the way. Louis calmly got out of the car and walked the few steps to the passenger entrance. This was on the side of bus opposite to where the driver was sitting. Louis noticed immediately that there was only one passenger on the bus.

As Louis made his way to the closed door, he gesticulated with his arms that the engine had died and was attempting to make it clear by shrugging his shoulders. He was no mechanic and therefore the car was there to stay. The driver shook his head frustrated by the whole episode, almost instantaneously Louis was on the bus. He pistol whipped the driver who was at once rendered unconscious. The man on the bus however reacted in a most unexpected manner, rather than hold his hands up appreciating the advantage Louis held by actually holding a gun, he stood up and charged straight at Louis yelling.

The smoke slowly drifted from the end of the barrel. The driver had fallen over one of the seats. He lay slumped in a heap on the floor. The blood from where the bullet had entered his temple trickled down towards the back of the bus.

"Hurry" Louis ordered van Rijn into the bus. "Get into that jacket. I'll put on the driver's hat and drive."

Several minutes later, the bus was slowly winding its way up the slope. Louis was calm. He had been in situations like this before, but he had other considerations this time. Sarah was never far from his thoughts. He was now again considering the possibility of her being inside the castle. He began to feel his pulse race as his heart beats reverberated through his entire body. He turned and looked at van Rijn. He looked lifeless. His eyes fixed as though now in a trance on the view through the front window.

"You must really want these paintings Marco," Louis was making reference to the intensity evident in van Rijn's facial expression.

"Let us just say I have waited a long time for this Louis." The response was calm yet chilling, he believed he was close to his objective and as a result his demeanour had changed. The friendliness had disappeared from his mannerisms. When he spoke he only slightly moved his head towards Louis and was now again fixed on a point through the window.

Louis had no reason to necessarily find anything wrong in van Rijn's actions. He too, in the final moments of a mission would find himself retreating into his own consciousness, focussing on what possibly lay ahead. He did this for several reasons, primarily to ensure there was no room for error, this in turn would maximise the probability of success, but also, at much more a sub-conscious perspective was the need to almost cleanse himself of any moral doubt prior to the execution. The need to remove emotion from his actions was as exacting as the event itself, but yet it was strange to see another going through the same ritual, as though looking at himself in a mirror.

The bus traversed down the other side of the slope. The first set of sentries were now in sight. Louis saw one of them look up the slope towards the bus. It was more of a nonchalant glance than a look of any real interest. If the sentries could just keep looking away, they could drive straight through.

Louis felt his hands tighten on the wheel as they turned the final corner. He tried to keep the bus at a steady speed for the fifty or so yards to the sentry post. The last few trips had resulted in the bus being waved through. Louis lowered the driver's cap and pulled his pistol from his pocket. He had taken the decision to attach a silencer to avoid any undue attention. Under the walls of the castle, unless there was one of the wall sentries looking over the parapet, any confrontation could pass without anyone noticing.

As it was the bus was waved straight through. "Yes" whispered van Rijn as the bus drove across the small bridge. They had managed to breach the walls of the castle with an old bus.

"Our own little Trojan horse," Louis remarked as he put his pistol back inside his jacket. He turned to van Rijn behind him. "You go to the main door and I'll carry your bag. That shouldn't look too suspicious."

They had parked the bus at the far end of the courtyard, with the other large cars. Whilst it wasn't obscured it was still hidden enough to avoid any unnecessary attention. Louis followed van Rijn, a couple of steps behind him. Should they be confronted by anyone speaking German, Louis wanted to ensure that van Rijn was the recipient of any questions. Notwithstanding such prudent action, he switched the bag to his other hand, took out his gun and placed into his jacket pocket, ready for immediate use if necessary.

Ahead of them stood a large imposing entrance to the castle itself. The door was open and the two men could see through straight into an internal courtyard. The inside appeared well lit, either by lanterns or torches. Natural daylight was not reaching the internal part of the castles. Without the artificial lighting, both men would have been able to feel a little more comfortable in the shadows, but it was highly unlikely that any visitor off the bus had not been expected and therefore met upon arrival.

Once past the door, van Rijn stopped. He turned to Louis and held out his hand for the bag. Louis saw in van Rijn's eyes that something had alarmed him. Whatever it was, it was something of which Louis was as of yet unaware.

"Danke," van Rijn said as he accepted the bag from Louis. Immediately it was obvious to him that van Rijn had spotted someone watching them and they were close.

"Comrade Tchourina, I welcome you to the Wolves Den. My name is Herr Hessler. I trust your journey here has not been too tiresome?"

"Niet, it has been more than comfortable. It is my undoubted pleasure to be here." For the next few moments a conversation ensued between the two men in Russian. As

Louis walked away without turning to look at either man, he couldn't help but be impressed by the speed at which van Rijn had jumped into character. The Dutchman had spent much time in the Soviet Union over the last twenty years on covert assignments, but that didn't prevent Louis appreciating another professional at work. But there was something that made Louis slow as he approached the door and therefore the cover of the shadows.

Hessler, the man that had greeted van Rijn, although he had yet to see his face, Louis immediately recognised that there something familiar about the man's voice. Once obscured by the shadows, Louis quickly and quietly leapt to his left just before he exited through the main door. He crouched down and looked back. He was by now twenty yards from where van Rijn and the man were standing. He peered intently at the man's face.

Louis' focus honed in. He saw at once that he was right. The man who had introduced himself as Hessler was The Scorpion. The light from one of the torches on the wall was now fully highlighting his face. It was unmistakable.

Louis' immediate response was to attack. He knew that by using the cover of the shadows he would be able to kill Hessler before he had any time to defend himself or raise the alarm. But if he did that he would not know for sure if Sarah was safe.

"Please Comrade Tchourina, follow me, to your room. The others have already arrived. We have been looking forward to our get together for some time now. The Master has been overjoyed at the support he has received." Hessler was grinning as he spoke.

"Herr Hessler, why do you call him Master?" Both men stopped walking and turned towards each other. "In Russia we are not used to such deference. Why not just call him by his name?" The question from van Rijn was disguised as though just a general question based upon his own curiosity. In reality the desire to ascertain who the 'Master' was almost overwhelming.

An awkward silence followed the question. Louis slowly leaned his head forward and slightly to one side. It was perhaps at this moment that the mysterious 'Master' would be uncloaked.

"Ha ha, I almost thought you were being serious. You sound like one of those communist pigs. Come, let us get you to your room. You will be required to attend the gathering in the Great Room at two o' clock.

Louis trailed them through to the other side of the courtyard. He followed the wall on the eastern side of the square, crouching as he moved towards the far end of the opening. As they left the courtyard the two men rose up a small stone staircase. Louis was only a matter of a few yards behind them. At the top of the staircase there was a small corridor with several further doors. The two men stopped at the final door on the right. Hessler pulled out a key, unlocked the door and move into the room, van Rijn followed him.

"I trust you will be comfortable," Hessler addressed van Rijn as he moved back towards the door.

"Don't move," ordered Louis. "Move over there and keep your mouth shut. Say a bloody word and I'll shoot you." Louis entered the room from the corridor and pushed Hessler back with his free hand, the other holding his gun.

Hessler looked at him with almost disbelief. He had expected a degree of determination from Louis to come looking for him and more than likely Sarah. He wouldn't have been at all surprised if their paths were to cross again at some point in the future, but here in the Wolves Den and so soon after their last meeting was a shock.

"Very enterprising Doctor. We have your colleague. I have since found out her real name, and of course you are the intrepid Louis Blue. It took us very little time to find out your identity." Hessler sneered as he said it. He appeared to take great pleasure from informing Louis that he knew their identities. But the fact that he had also been outwitted was perhaps the most displeasing aspect of this episode.

"You know my name?" It was now Louis' turn to look a little surprised.

"Of course Louis, or should I say Lucifer Blue?" Hessler grinned. He was now feeling a little more comfortable having turned the table a little. "A friend was very forthcoming with the information when you began to poke your nose in dangerous places. I didn't think you were a doctor anyway. You hardly look the educated type."

"Abel's dead." came the response and within moments Hessler was in a crumpled heap on the floor. Louis had pistol whipped him across the side of the face, the blood slowly started to trickle from the side of his mouth. "Get up now you bastard and tell me what all these people arriving on the buses are doing here?" Louis paused for a moment. There was something far more urgent he needed to ask. "What you have done with Sarah?" Louis assumed that if Hessler knew his name, then Abel must have also told him Sarah's real name too.

"Ah, so I was right on that little matter too. You hardly appeared to be enjoying only a professional relationship. It was your eyes and your actions I'm afraid, gives it away every time. But you said Abel is dead, I have no doubt that means something to you idiot, but it means nothing to me."

Louis lifted the gun again, poised, as though to strike the man beneath him for the second time. Hessler raised his right arm to defend himself, but Louis pulled the blow up short. Instead he attached the silencer to the gun and pressed the end of the barrel up against Hessler' forehead.

"I'll count to three," Louis was genuinely ready to kill him. He had believed there to be only a slim chance that Sarah was not yet dead, but he had received the confirmation he so desperately wanted to hear, that she still very much alive. Irrespective of this, he had been tortured by the uncertainty of the last few days. Without any second thoughts, he would enjoy this particular kill.

Hessler thought for a moment. He focussed his eyes on the gun up against his face, looked to the ceiling and sighed. "Okay, you'll never get away from here alive anyway. She's down in one of the cells below the castle."

"I got in didn't I and surely you didn't expect that. You plainly underestimate me. Of course I'll get out. Marco, do you want to ask him about the paintings?" Louis' sense of relief began to overwhelm him, Sarah was alive and she was nearby. He felt a surge of strength enter his body as the adrenalin started to pump through his veins.

"What about the men? They've been turning up all morning. What on earth is going on in this place?" Louis' question was of course of secondary concern. Yet nonetheless he was intrigued. There was something quite mysterious about the arrivals that morning.

"They are followers. They believe that the red hordes need to be stopped once and for all." Hessler banged his fist into the table beside him. "Your country and your allies believe they were defeating evil in the last war. You are completely mistaken if you believe that the Communists don't pose an even greater threat. These men merely understand the importance of using every available resource to stem the tide."

"But there can be no more than fifty men in the whole castle. What do you believe such a small number are capable of doing?" Louis shook his head, the question was delivered more as a damning indictment.

Hessler's laughter was a measured response. It was just enough to highlight that there was obviously more to the collection of these individuals than otherwise seemed apparent from what had been witnessed this morning from the top of the hill.

"Those men," Hessler emphasised his reference to 'men'. It was as though merely referring to them in this way was doing them a great disservice. He continued, "are some of the most powerful men in the world. They have been coming here on a regular basis for the last few years to meet and obtain their orders from their Master. It is not in the rooms of Westminster or Washington where the fight is being won against the Communists. It is here, right in this very castle where the strategies to ensure the defeat of the Soviet Union and similarly perverse nations are drawn up." Hessler was now revelling in his role.

Not for the first time, Louis felt his curiosity get the better of him. He was actually finding it all extremely interesting.

"But I'm still at a loss as to who these men are and what these men actually do when they leave here."

"As I said they are incredibly powerful, resourceful individuals. For a long time many of them were against us. Perhaps at that stage we all had different perspectives. They were driven by natural nationalistic tendencies. But now these men leave here, they go back to their banks, their institutions, their companies and they do all they can to ensure the organisation they are associated with assists our cause. They all help. From the smallest donation, which this year was a sum of several million dollars, to the provision of 'disciples' of our belief, they are spread throughout the whole world. They ensure that whenever an opportunity arises to cause maximum disruption to our enemy, they take advantage of it." Hessler paused, thereby allowing Louis the opportunity to interject.

"So, I guess you're telling me, you have your own well funded set of fanatics, looking to destroy anyone or anything that doesn't share the same ideology. That seems to ring a bell, look what happened the last time you tried that. I'm interested, are they all as hell bent on destruction as the last lot?"

"You think you are funny, stupid man, but you are not. Using my alias of The Scorpion, I was able to cause more damage to the growth of the Communists in South East Asia than any invading army ever could. Everywhere you look in the world, Communism is on the march. If it wasn't for me and those like me, millions would die and our society would very soon come to an end."

It was now Louis' turn to laugh. "Just seems a little ironic, coming from someone like you." The point had been made.

For the last few minutes van Rijn had appeared preoccupied. He had been staring out of the window into the central courtyard as though looking for someone or something. Louis had assumed he had merely been keeping watch.

"Er, yes of course," van Rijn was hardly sanguine in his response, nevertheless he continued. "Where are the missing Rembrandts?"

Hessler chuckled. "So you are still looking for your ten Rembrandts. You are both fools then. Of course there aren't ten missing Rembrandts. If this is why you are here then you have wasted your time."

Louis looked at van Rijn. He was expecting a furious outburst, but instead van Rijn just lowered his head. Louis was now more confused than at any time in the whole mission. Perhaps this was some sort of ploy of van Rijn's to feign indifference to the answer. Louis could sense however that there was something not quite right. The expression, the lack of conviction in the question and reaction to the answer left Louis somewhat bemused.

Louis looked at van Rijn, "Marco," suddenly Louis stopped. There were footsteps coming up the stairs at the end of the hallway. Louis gently shut the door, took the key and slowly locked the door. Ten seconds later there was a light tap at the door.

"Hello, is anybody in there?" The accent was heavy. It was American. "Comrade Tchourina, good buddy, it's me, Rick Fenton."

Louis placed his finger over his mouth and again pointed the gun at Hessler's temple. He shook his head as to emphasise to say nothing. There was silence for several moments before the American turned and walked back down the corridor.

"Why is there an American here and who were all those people that I saw turning up this morning?" This was not of primary interest to Louis, but he had allowed his curiosity to get the better of him.

Hessler just smiled and shook his head. He was by now annoying Louis with just about everything he said. Louis was tempted to crack the gun over his head for a second time, but he was now wasting precious moments, Sarah was downstairs in a cell and he needed to find her.

"Right, take us to her Hessler. One false move, one word out of line and I will put a bullet through your head. You can trust me on that and know I'll enjoy doing it." Louis lifted the pistol again to remind him.

Hessler shook his head suggesting it was a futile exercise, but nonetheless he could see Louis and his accomplice were determined.

"Okay follow me." The three men left the room, van Rijn, followed by Hessler and then Louis who had the barrel squeezed up against Hessler's back.

The men reached the courtyard. The lack of direct light again favoured them. They were able to stick closely to the dark shadows against the walls and continued to the far corner Hessler had gestured towards. At the corner there was a small opening that had old stone stairs going up a well lit stairwell. There were also some stone stairs that spiralled downwards but nothing could be seen looking by down. It was far too dark. Again Hessler nodded, this time in the direction of the darkness.

The stairs were very tight. Feet had obviously been a lot smaller at the time of the castle's construction. All three men could feel their toes dangling over the edge of each step and the descent was steep. One small slip could be potentially disastrous. Louis reminded Hessler that he was still very much their captive with a little extra pressure from the end of the pistol.

After two minutes of descending the staircase, a little flickering light illuminated the stairs below them. They were now almost at the bottom and could see a small corridor ahead of them. It was lit by torches, but it was very cold and very dark, not the kind of place Louis wanted to imagine Sarah in. At the end of end of the corridor there were four more steps that led into a chamber with three doors in the middle of each wall. In the middle of the chamber was a table with a man sitting with a candle and an open book on the table. He appeared to be a guard.

He looked to the three men not showing any visible signs of alarm, awaiting some form of command, Louis pulled the gun from behind Hessler and shot the man twice, once in the heart and once in the head. He quickly searched the body and found some keys. They had the appearance of being more than likely able to unlock these large doors.

Louis gently knocked on the first door, "Sarah are you there?" There was no response. He crossed the room and knocked on the second door repeating the same question, this time he heard a shuffle of feet from behind the door.

"Hello, who is it? Is that you Louis?" With the utmost haste, Louis started to frantically insert the keys one by one till he felt the lock turn. He pulled back the cell door.

"Oh Louis, thank God, I thought I was going to die." Sarah threw her arms around Louis' neck, he was not used to affection of any kind, but equally he was not used to feeling such jubilation. He squeezed her tightly and kissed the side of her face, then her forehead.

"Quick you two, hurry," van Rijn implored them to follow him, but first he turned towards Hessler, pulled out his gun and fired. Hessler slumped to the floor. He made no sound. The bullet had entered his brain and death was immediate. Sarah turned and pushed her face as hard as she could into Louis' chest. Louis hated van Rijn for letting Sarah see him kill Hessler in cold blood, but he knew also that Hessler had served his purpose and escaping would be difficult enough without having to consider Hessler too.

The three of them made their way back up the stairs. There was still no sign of any guards. It was becoming a little disconcerting. They entered the courtyard and again followed the outer rim of the wall. Suddenly there was a mighty whoosh. All around them large electrical lights illuminated the entire square. At nearly every window on the floor above them was a guard aiming a gun at them. Instinctively they raised their arms.

Several moments passed, nothing was said and no one moved. They then heard a door creak and to their left, a large imposing door began to slowly open inwards. There was darkness from within, but they could see several figures beginning to emerge.

First came two guards, armed and with their eyes looking down the sights of the gun barrel. Louis knew that if he was to try anything he would be mown down in an instant. Behind them, a darkened silhouette moved towards the opening.

Louis looked at the man. His stare began as one of curiosity as to who the man was. This expression however began to slowly change to one of astonishment. Louis was momentarily stunned by what he saw. There was nothing that could have prepared him for this sight. Despite the years Louis immediately recognised the person standing in front of him. There could be no doubt that the man standing before him would be the person referred to as the Master. The man who stood before him was old. He wore a black suit and a similar coloured polo neck sweater. Physically, he was broad and somewhat overweight, his appearance suggesting that he may have struggled with his own mobility. It was also noticeable he was not comfortable standing straight, evident due the fact that every few seconds he would move his weight from foot to foot. As with many older men in their latter years, he would have appeared to have developed a stoop, in turn the process of standing was therefore taking its toll. His hair was grey yet obviously groomed. He looked at his audience with his head turned slightly to one side, his sight assisted by a monocle.

"You are intruders in my home," the man standing in front Louis, Marco and Sarah scornfully addressed them.

"How can we be intruders in the home of a man that has been dead for over twenty years?" Louis responded.

The man laughed out loud, Louis' reply had obviously amused him. The roar echoed around the entire courtyard. Sarah looked puzzled. It was obvious Louis knew who the man was. She moved her mouth towards van Rijn's ear.

"Who is it?" Sarah whispered, Louis and the man were engaged with each other and she hoped van Rijn could respond without attracting too much attention.

"That Sarah, is Reichmarshal Herman Goering," he almost shouted the response. "This is the Nazi pig who murdered my wife."

Sarah looked and blinked at the man. Since nineteen forty six the world had believed him dead. She remembered reading about him at school, he had been at one time Hitler's named successor and the most senior Nazi to authorise the 'Final Solution' in writing, but she also knew that after his capture following Hitler's suicide, he had been convicted of crimes against humanity at The Nuremberg Trials. Sentenced to execution, he then committed suicide with a vial of poison, or so she and just about everybody else thought.

She froze, rooted to the very spot she stood upon. There are those who imagine living history, what it may be like to come to face to face with a person from the past, a morbid curiosity maybe. Yet nothing could probably ready someone should it ever actually happen. The questions that Sarah may have wanted to ask had she been prepared however were simply not forthcoming. Maybe because to imagine such scenarios, they are normally round a dinner table, informal affairs perhaps, fear and hate play no part of the event, but for now in Sarah's and Abel's case, their was an abundance of both. The questions would have to wait.

"Yes, you are right you fool. I am Goering. Who you are is of no relevance to me, but why do you say I killed your wife? I have never killed anyone's wife, not knowingly anyway," again his laughter reverberated around the courtyard, "perhaps I squashed her," several of his men grinned.

Marco van Rijn looked to the floor and slowly began to weep. The attempt at humour had passed him by. His thoughts were focused on the past and the pain in his face was evident. Even the strongest men have an Achilles heel.

"Your men came to my house one night during the war, they were looking for treasure because of my name. They took a Rembrandt and when I tried to stop them they shot my wife. They were working on your orders." Distraught, van Rijn struggled with his words, trying to stem the flood of tears streaming down his face.

Louis looked at van Rijn. There was only one Rembrandt painting. "All this for one painting?" The question directed at van Rijn was borne almost out of desperation. But Sarah, sensitive to the heartache Marco had obviously endured over the years, forgot her fear for a moment, turned and scowled at Louis.

"No Louis," van Rijn replied, "for revenge. He murdered my wife."

"Gentlemen, gentlemen, I have heard enough for now. Take them back to the cells. I have guests to attend to." Goering turned out walked back through the open doorway.

As the three were searched for weapons, Louis turned to van Rijn. "Why did you make up the story about the ten Rembrandts Marco?"

"Because imagine I had told you I had always believed Hermann Goering was still alive and that I wanted to kill him out of revenge for the death of my wife. Your government would never have helped me. I needed a believable reason to get me here today. If people high up in your establishment had known why I wanted to enlist their help, they would have declined, not only because they didn't care, but more likely, because it was not in their interest that the truth should ever be known. Louis, have you not wondered why Abel was helping them and not you?"

Louis shook his head. There had indeed been a web of intrigue surrounding the whole episode. There were those who he had believed to be friends who had in fact been working against him all along and now one of the most infamous Nazis was holding them prisoner. Nothing would now surprise him. "No, tell me." Louis replied.

"Because since the war nearly every successive government in both your country and America has known of Goering's existence. They know because they planned his escape. When the Allies found his first stash of stolen art treasures near Hitler's 'Eagle Nest' he realised his position had actually been strengthened. He figured that rather than be executed with much of his wealth hidden forever, he could broker a deal. He told them he had a much greater collection of money, jewellery, art and other prized assets hidden somewhere in Europe. In return for allowing him to live he would periodically return much of what he had taken, sometimes however at a fair price. In short he blackmailed them."

Louis was stunned. Everything he had read over the last twenty years regarding the war had been damning vitriol aimed at the defeated Nazi war machine. To think that all along the Western governments had in fact been protecting one of its leading members was almost comical to Louis. He had been provided with many enemies of the state as targets over the years, surely, he thought someone would have ordered this one.

"He must be a particularly large benefactor," Louis sensed the hypocritical injustice of the arrangement, but even more so, he remembered why Marco was here. He squeezed Sarah's hand and felt a genuine pity for van Rijn.

All three were placed in the same cell. This particular room was slightly bigger than the one that had held Sarah. There was an external window, albeit it was barred.

"I still don't get it," Louis was shaking his head and looking genuinely puzzled. " I can't believe they allowed Herman Goering of all people to escape?"

"My friend, it was probably a little bit of greed and a little bit of desperation," replied van Rijn. "Following the end of the war, most countries including yours had been financially devastated by the costs of the previous six years. The States had pledged millions to rebuilding Europe and the old colonial Far East. If you think about it, it makes complete sense. What's the one thing that both your country and the Americans fear more than anything?"

"The Communists," replied Louis.

"Exactly," van Rijn looked pleased, "so following on from that, if there was an individual who could pledge an enormous amount of riches to a 'cause' in return for being allowed to live in secrecy, this could provide a buffer and assist in the battle against the spread of Communism. He realised, there was a significant likelihood that his demands would be met and this was exactly what had happened.

"What about all the people turning up earlier today, despite what Hessler said? Do you think most of them are just simply old Nazis in hiding?" Louis seemingly forgetting the predicament they were in, appeared genuinely enthralled by the momentous chain of events, it was a re-writing of history and he was witnessing it first hand.

"I doubt it," replied van Rijn, " it's much more likely they are his agents, acting as the enforcers within a global syndicate. During the war he was always regarded as a tyrannical megalomaniac. Astonishing as it may seem, he appears to have got his wish, his influence is stretching probably further than if the Nazis had actually won. All that was necessary at Nuremberg was for a plausible reason to be given as to why he could not face a public execution. Some cleverly staged photographs and medical reports instead and one of the biggest cover ups of all time was put in motion."

"Well what the hell shall we do, is he the enemy or not?" responded Louis, "I've spent much of the last ten years killing Communists for other people, is he really doing anything different to us? Louis looked almost ashamedly at van Rijn as he spoke, he realised immediately the mistake.

"Say what you will Louis, but that man killed my wife and hundreds of thousands of others. Yet our powerful leaders allowed him to live and to thrive, it is as though the past had never happened. I will kill him Louis, that I swear. With that van Rijn sat down against one of the walls, closed his eyes and lowered his head.

Louis put his arm gently round Sarah's shoulder and looked into her eyes, he could still see the fear, they were together but her lot had not really changed, her only hope was now caged up beside her

"Sarah, I promise you, everything is going to be fine."

"You promise Louis?" Sarah had every confidence in Louis but her response had a hint of desperation in it. Louis just nodded, he hated being trapped.

Nightfall came and went, there were no visitors, no food or drink and apart from the odd distant sound of footsteps, there was very little to compare with the excitement of the previous day. All this however was about to change.

At around mid morning, Louis heard from afar the approach of several people. The door opened and in walked three guards.

"You two, come with us." the guard who had given the command pointed at Louis and Sarah.

"What about me?" van Rijn asked nervously, rising to his feet.

"Oh yes, you I almost forgot. The Master was so upset about the story of your wife," the guard paused for a second, "that he feels you should join her." With that the guard raised his gun and fired. Four bullets ripped into van Rijn's body and sent him crashing backwards against the wall.

Sarah screamed. Louis stood frozen to the spot, the fury welled inside him to volcanic proportions. He was ready to let loose his own brand of hell. Within seconds three more men lay dead on the floor. One with a bullet to the forehead, one with a broken neck and one with Louis' hidden blade thrust into the top of his skull.

Louis retrieved his knife, he looked across to Sarah. For the first time, he had not considered her safety. His actions had been an immediate response borne out of emotion and the rage was a result of the death of a friend. She had witnessed Louis at his professional apex. She knew him capable of these actions, she had read his file after all, but this was a man who she believed she loved as he loved her.

His actions shocked her, perhaps she had tried to ignore the thoughts of him doing such things. But Sarah had just been witness to Lucifer's retribution. It was chillingly effective. Nevertheless, she had dropped to the floor when the onslaught began as Louis grabbed the gun which had killed van Rijn. She was breathing heavily and appeared to be about to go into shock.

"Everything is fine Sarah, I promised you everything would be okay. These men were bad men, now come on we've got to get out of here." Louis picked up the keys and moved the bodies, including van Rijn's to the near wall, obscuring them away from any prying eyes which may look through the small slot in the door. He put his arm around Sarah and led her out the room, locking the door behind him as they left.

The two of them began to climb the stairs. Fortunately the cells were deep enough under the castle to be almost completely soundproof. The sound of the guns had been muted. Therefore it would be safe to assume at this stage that they were still undetected. Although, Louis also knew that the men who had come to get them would soon be missed. If they were to escape they would have to move quickly.

"Louis, how are we going to get out?" Sarah whispered.

"The same way I got in. I used one of the vehicles in the courtyard, I left the keys inside the wheel arches." At this point Louis stopped in his tracks and pondered for a moment before continuing. "But first I have to do something."

"Oh Louis, please let's get away from here, I'm afraid."

"I know darling, I know," he slowly moved her towards him and gently kissed the side of her face. She looked into his eyes and smiled, she took strength from the confidence that they exuded. He had kept her alive to this point, she had no reason to fear that he couldn't continue to do so.

"I'm going to take you to the bus that I came in on Sarah. I want you to lay low at the back and not make a sound. I won't be long," Louis held her hand and led her along the outer wall of the courtyard, keeping low and ducking under the occasional window.

Within several minutes they were at the bus. "Louis please tell me where you are going." Sarah was now more concerned for Louis than she was for herself. The bus would provided a sanctuary out of harm's way till Louis' return, there were many other cars parked nearby. For now it seemed to be one of the safest places within the castle.

"Sarah, several people I have come to know well have died. They have been killed as a result of what's going on in this castle. Yet it's not revenge I seek, I just need to do something that should have been done many years ago. Inside that castle is a man who quite simply should never have been allowed to live."

"Louis," Sarah replied, "why don't we just get out and tell our people that he's here?"

"Because it's our people who put him here in the first place, they cannot be trusted to do the right thing." Louis turned and walked away, as he did so he pointed to the bus, beckoning Sarah to get inside.

Back within the main courtyard, Louis went straight to the door through which he had seen Goering enter. He turned the handle. It made a slight squeak. The door was probably hundreds of years old but remarkably well intact. Thankfully for Louis the hinges had been recently oiled.

Once inside, Louis' eyes began to adjust to the darkness. In front of him was an old stone staircase which had a deep purple, almost regal carpet covering most of the stone. Looking down Louis could also see the emblem of the eagle, long associated with empires. This particular eagle was a hallmark associated with the Third Reich. Acting almost as a guide to his target, slowly Louis began to ascend the stairs.

After two flights the stairs came to an end. There was a long hallway. He looked right and could see on either side running along the walls, several small doors. The lighting was dimmer to that side and whilst that afforded more protection from being spotted, the brighter lights to the other end were far more likely to lead to his prey. Louis stood hidden in the darkened doorway to the left of the stairs for several moments, listening and waiting for something to assist him, all was deathly quiet until suddenly the largest door at the end of the hallway on the right swung open. A man hurriedly left the room and headed towards the stairs, his face revealed a distressed expression.

"Tell those idiots to bring them here now, I have people waiting for me." a voice from inside the room shouted after the man. Louis waited for the man to scamper down the stairs then calmly walked down to the other end of the corridor. The door had been left slightly ajar by the departing man.

Louis entered into what immediately appeared to be a formal living room. He had earlier taken one of the guard's pistols and now drew it from his pocket. The room was in keeping with the more grandiose elements of the castle, the walls were draped with fine oil paintings and the furniture antique, it's opulent yet comfortable feel, suggested much time was spent in here.

Sitting down facing a roaring fire and with the back of his head showing over the top of one of the large chairs was Goering.

"Stand up," Louis closed the door behind him and locked it.

Goering slowly turned around, looking genuinely surprised he then smiled as he rose to his feet. "Very impressive young man. Are you intending to kill all my men?"

"Shut up, you are not in a position to be funny now old man," Louis was thinking of Marco and his wife, of Abel and the hopeless position he had found himself in, but more importantly he thought of the danger that Sarah had been put in. "I am here to kill you."

"Now why would you want to do that? What will you gain from my death? But perhaps more importantly, what will you lose?" Goering despite his predicament was still the master statesman, his response was calm and unhurried.

"Because of you I have friends who are now dead. You in your time have been responsible for the death of many thousands, you are an animal and it is now your turn to be slaughtered, this is my final solution."

Goering shook his head slowly from side to side. "Young man you may be right, I was what I was in the past, but that is behind me. Your government has found it prudent to forgive me, I'm sure you can too. Lucifer I know more about you than you think. We are very similar you and I and you can't even see it."

Louis looked puzzled, he had expected to merely walk into the room, exact punishment for crimes committed and then leave, but somehow he was being dragged into a conversation he had no desire for.

"Think for a moment what it is you do, you are a puppet for the State, you carry out their commands, no questions asked, but all you are really doing is keeping everyone safe. I'm sure your adventures are exciting and varied, but you spend much of your time stopping the Communists from spreading their evil disease. So why are we so different?"

Louis for the first time since entering the room looked away. He desperately searched for a cutting response to repudiate Goering's suggestion, but he struggled. There was no doubting the fact that much of what he did had been simply to ensure the balance of power didn't lean to far towards the other side. Nevertheless he felt obliged to respond.

"You have murdered thousands of innocent people, my actions are merely to defend my country's way of life. I am no great patriot, but I can see the sense in balance. I do what I do because I am who I am and I do it very well, but you, you killed thousands of innocents for the sake of your vanity.

"Like you Louis, I was merely following orders," Goering again grinned as he spoke.

"Don't you dare, don't you bloody dare." Louis walked towards the old man and pushed the end of the gun into his temple. For the first time since he could remember, at the point of squeezing the trigger, Louis faltered. He looked deep into Goering's eyes, he saw no fear, but what he did see was the frightening truth, there really was very little to separate them. Louis was sure many innocents had probably died at his hands over the years and now Goering himself was being used as a similar puppet, acting both as a financier and leader to groups and individuals around the world united against Communism, but doing so with the express knowledge and backing of the West.

Louis took the gun away from Goering's head and sat down. He was shocked with himself that he had been unable to pull the trigger. The fact was, the man to an extent had been correct in his aspersions, whilst hardly brothers in arms, they were both tasked with achieving the same end game.

"Louis, the Communists are our shared enemies. We will never be alike in many ways, but we will also always be the same." Goering nodded as though looking for approval for his comment.

"I have no enemies," Louis' response was as immediate as it was true, "but what I don't understand is why if my government has always known of your existence, they sent me on this wild goose chase? It would have been far simpler to have vetoed the whole mission from the outset." Louis was now remembering the comments of Colonel Mallory and the Minister.

"It is to your credit that you got this far. No-one would have ever expected you to find us, but perhaps you should also know that for security reasons there are very few people who know of my existence. Despite my earlier denial, I knew who Marco van Rijn was when we met in the courtyard. I have made many enemies over the years and of course they would want me dead. Equally however there is a need to keep my survival secret. It would be calamitous for your Government to release not only knowledge of my existence but that they have supported me for the last twenty years."

Louis just simply shook his head, "and Colonel Mallory, was he aware too?"

"Mallory, no, he has no idea. As I said very few people know I am here. One day I'm sure the world will know that I survived the fake suicide, but till then I will continue to do what I do, that is, if you let me live.

Louis felt sickened, perhaps one of the most evil men of the century had managed to debate the logic of his actions and Louis had not been able to find a compelling point with which to disagree. The comfort however came from the knowledge debate was not his forte. He looked at his gun, Louis knew he rarely lost an argument.

"Will you let us leave here alive?" Louis asked.

"Of course, if you let me live." responded Goering, realising that the imminent danger had now passed.

There had been many occasions in the past when Louis had been asked to trust someone, more often than not when his life depended upon it, but he was not a man to take unnecessary risks and with his and Sarah's situation being as perilous as it was at this moment. Now was not a time to discover whether the word of a man generally held responsible for the deaths of many thousands was honourable.

"I'm afraid I don't believe you," Louis' words were drowned out as he brought an ornamental candlestick holder crashing into the back of Goering's head. There were two loud thuds, the first from the impact on the back of the skull and the second as Goering fell as though he had been shot. Louis stood over him for a matter of a few seconds. It was still tempting to exact revenge at this stage, but he had been confused by the discussion, there were elements of truth in the similarities suggested and with his clarity somewhat distorted, for the second time Louis took the decision to allow him to live.

Almost immediately, Louis' thoughts returned to safety of Sarah. He dragged the unconscious body behind a sofa. Unless somebody was to look around the back of it, the likelihood of Goering's body being located before he actually awoke would be extremely unlikely. It had been a forceful clump which apart from satisfying the immediate requirement would give Louis plenty of time to collect Sarah and escape.

Nevertheless there was equally no reason to hang about, he marched briskly to the door and made his way towards the stairs.

"Damn," he whispered to himself. Looking down the stairs to the floor below he saw the top of the man's head who minutes earlier had left the room with Goering's orders bellowing behind him. Louis realised that it was more than likely that the man was returning to report that the men had gone missing and a request for the general alarm to be raised.

Louis moved back around the corner, hidden and away from the staircase. He widened his stance and crouched. As the man reached the top of the stairs Louis lurched forward at lightening speed, his knuckles of his right hand nearly took the man's head clear off his shoulders as his body landed seven stairs behind where he been momentarily standing. The contorted positioning of his head left Louis in no doubt he was dead.

Time was now considerably more of a concern than it had been, Louis guessed that it would not be too long before the body would be found on the staircase. Within minutes he was back at the bus.

Wasting no time, he gestured to Sarah to keep her head down. She didn't move, she had spent the last ten minutes convinced that Louis was probably dead and that she would soon be discovered. His reappearance made her almost shout with exuberant joy. The end to this particular nightmare was almost in sight, but Louis' demeanour highlighted that they were still in imminent danger. She therefore did exactly as directed as the bus moved off slowly towards the sentry post.

It was highly likely that the arrivals and departures of the vehicles were scheduled. This was evident in that whilst entering the castle they had been waved through, this time the two sentries came out to meet the bus. There was no urgency on the part of the guards, they were there primarily to ensure that nothing got in, less of a concern was people trying to escape.

Louis brought the bus to a stop and calmly opened the door. The two men smiled and nodded, but their futile attempts to try and reach for their guns were in vain as both men looked down to Louis' hand. He fired twice, the silencer on the gun making no more than a hissing sound. Both men received a bullet in the forehead and slumped forward onto the bottom step of the bus. Praying that none of the other sentries had been alerted by their unscheduled departure, Louis dragged both men onto the bus and lay them in the aisle, Sarah winced as she turned her head away from the bodies.

Louis drove the bus forward at a gentle pace, a sudden acceleration would bring unnecessary attention. They crossed the small bridge and once out of the castle, Louis afforded a little more power to help the bus up the winding slope. As they reached the top of the hill, Louis looked into the rear view mirror, he could see Sarah lying down, her face pressed into the seat.

"It's okay, we're out." Louis gently placed his hand on her shoulder. "We'll leave the bus here, hurry though, I have a car a short distance down the road parked in the trees." Sarah took a deep breath and looked out of the rear window. It was over, she was free, smiling she grabbed Louis by the hand.

The two returned to England. The past few weeks had been perilous and in many respects a waste of time. There had never been any paintings, at least not the ten or so Rembrandts that Marco had let everyone believe had been stolen. But as futile as the mission had been, the fact that he was now party to one of the darkest secrets of the Second World War provided Louis with a comprehension as to what it had all been about. But he needed some kind of explanation, people he had known and trusted had betrayed or lied to him and now they were dead.

They made their way to the Ministry, Louis believing that an appointment with the Minister in the circumstances would hardly be necessary. After several minutes waiting they were shown in. Hardly unexpected, Colonel Mallory had arrived before them.

"Louis I'm dreadfully sorry, I promise you I didn't know the truth until this morning." The Colonel looked genuinely apologetic as he spoke.

"I know Colonel. The Nazi told me himself that you knew nothing of his existence." Louis and Sarah sat down as he spoke. They both appreciated that this time it would be more than a fleeting visit.

"Why Minister, why did you not tell us?" Louis looked straight at the Minister as he asked the question. He had no problem with dangerous missions, but this time Sarah could have been killed and all because Goering had been allowed to live. Morally that didn't rest very well with Louis, the British Government allowing its own subjects to die so that a Nazi killer could remain alive and in hiding.

"Louis," the Minister replied with a sigh, "there was very little we could do. We never believed for one moment anything would come of this. We believed Marco was sincere when he made his request. Of course we never considered Goering to be still alive. Why would anyone who wasn't party to the secret? For those that knew, there was never any suggestion that you could be successful, but you managed to follow the trail, all the way to the end. If the truth is to be known, no-one has ever looked for him before as his suicide was never questioned."

"But why did we let him live?" Louis looked utterly dejected by the manner in which the conversation was unfolding. "Surely there are better ways of defending us against the Soviet Bloc than allowing a Nazi Reichsmarshal to live in opulence, hiding among the people whose lives he helped destroy."

"Louis, the cover-up of his suicide came as a shock to me too, but think about it, the threat from the Communists is real. They mass their armies at the door of Western Europe and they aim their nuclear missiles at every city in this country. I can assure you Louis, we are a significantly more concerned about the future than we are the past. The Minister had become unusually animated, he sensed that whilst the horrors of the last war still left their scar, there was now an undeniable logic to his argument.

Louis just lowered his head. His life had been non-existent for so long. His only reason for living was to stop other people from continuing the same benefit. Yet here he was, dejected by the unmistakeable truth that one of the most despised men of the previous quarter of a century was helping his country against a new enemy.

"Well what do we now then?" Louis asked standing to his feet. We know everything. Can we be trusted?"

"Of course, you both have been to Hell and back, please don't think for a moment that we don't value you Louis, or you Sarah. However, there are those who control our State who just simply had to do what they had to do." The Minister nodded as though requiring affirmation of his last comment.

The Colonel interrupted. "There's bound to be a promotion in it for you old boy."

"For the love of God Colonel. Do you think I care? Promotion to what anyway? I'm not in the army, or at least I wasn't before this whole sorry mess started." He looked across to Sarah. "If it's okay with you both I think I'll say my goodbye."

The Minister stood to his feet. "Goodbye Louis and good luck. We'll be in touch, oh and Happy Christmas, its tomorrow you know?"

Louis walked towards the door, looking at Sarah. He realised that without asking her, he had expected her to leave with him. He stopped beside her chair and gave her a gentle smile. She held out her hand and together they left the Ministry, both hoping this visit to be their last.

For the next few days the two of them endeavoured to do as little as possible. There were no plans as such to administer, yet despite this they were busy. Perhaps they were trying to assert normality into their existence, a life that at least one of them had never known. Sarah's flat in Bayswater was put up for sale. They rented a small flat in an exclusive part of Chelsea and without significant discussion as to either their relationship or their future, they just enjoyed the opportunity to spend time together. They spent Christmas day walking along the Embankment. They even managed to scrape some food together from the small shops on Edgware Road. They spent this particular Christmas cold and tired but together.

At the weekend Sarah had suggested they visit Covent Garden. She had always loved London life in action. The street entertainers, cafes and market stalls had made this a magical place for her as a child. Her parents had brought her back to London after the war and for many of her formative years she had seen the City in a way that it is sometimes best viewed, through a child's eyes.

"You know Louis, I believe things haven't been exactly in our favour since we met, but I really must tell you that I have honestly never been as happy as I am at this moment." Sarah put her arm round the back of Louis' head and kissed him on the lips.

Louis place both arms around her shoulders and squeezed her in tightly. His thoughts focussing on the irony of his last few months. Maybe the thing that he feared the most, that there was in fact a God, could perhaps provide the answer. How else could he explain that just at the time he felt as though his soul had ceased to exist, an angel had been delivered. He smiled and then in turn kissed her back.

"Let's eat Louis, I'm hungry." They had been walking for hours and it was still bitterly cold. "I know a small restaurant by St Martin's. I used to go there sometimes after I'd been to the art galleries. Louis raised an eyebrow, art galleries were something that for now were completely off the agenda.

The restaurant was not as small as Louis had expected. It had two floors and an unmistakeable French feel. It was almost full and that in itself provided an atmosphere. This part of London had many places to eat, yet restaurants such as this one were still not commonplace. The café was the most common form of diner and therefore a trip to this particular establishment would be regarded by most as a treat, Louis was no different. The customers were a mixture of pre-theatre diners and those like the two of them, just hungry people trying to get out of the cold.

After about five minutes the waiter appeared. He asked them if they would like a drink and passed them the menu. "May I have a whisky please?" responded Louis. "The lady would like a," he looked at Sarah and waited.

"I'll have a gin and tonic if I may?" Sarah replied taking her cue.

"Of course Madame." the waiter left to get their drinks.

"Well what are going to do Sarah? This is a fantastic, I'm seeing a part of life that I never knew existed but at some point we're going to have to make a plan. We'll need to find a jobs and decide where we're going to live. What about us? Are we going to live together soon and what about marriage, do you think we should?"

Sarah started to quietly giggle. Both had spent nearly a week since leaving the Ministry privately thinking all of these things, but because of necessity more than anything else, they had said nothing. There were things that simply needed doing not saying. But here and now Louis had managed to ask all the questions that mattered in the space of a few brief seconds. She reached over and held his hand.

"Oh Louis, you are so sweet, I love you so much." Louis grinned like an excited schoolboy. Nervously he looked down at the table.

"For you Madame." The waiter had spared his further blushes by returning with the drinks, "and for you Monsieur. I'll be over in a few moments to take your order."

They both grinned. Whatever had happened in Louis' past was now well and truly behind him. Life was now all about the future. At last all the things that he had considered beyond him, were now possible.

"Tell me Louis, Lucifer is not your real name is it?" Sarah leant towards him as she spoke. "The files only had so much about you. If I'm planning to spend the rest of my life with you, don't you think you should tell me your name?"

Louis leant back in his chair, smiled and now looked to the ceiling, he composed himself. In truth, it had been so many years since his true name had passed his lips that he had to convince himself that not only was he was about to do the right thing, but he also had to ensure that it was the correct name. His true identity, or the little he knew of it was his last line of defence, the fact that no-one really knew who he was or where he came from, was very soon about to change.

As he lowered his head back down, he heard a glass smash. He looked across at Sarah, her hands were stretched out across the table. She was obviously in a great deal of discomfort. Beginning to struggle with her breathing, her eyes were starting to roll upwards. Louis jumped up, he shouted at the top of his voice. "Quick get a doctor. Waiter. Where is that damn waiter? Will someone please call for a bloody doctor." He leapt to her side. "Don't panic Sarah, it will be alright, where is it hurting?"

"Louis, it's burning, inside me I can feel it burning." By now Sarah was starting to convulse. Louis had seen this many times before. He was fully aware as to the order of events. Normally being in close contact with the other victims too, but on those occasions he had been the cause of the agony. Sarah had been poisoned and there was very little he could do.

"Sarah, listen to me. You're going to go to sleep soon darling and when you wake up the pain will be gone. I want you to remember that I love you very much and that I will be with you very soon." Sarah's head turned slowly towards him. She attempted to smile and respond with a nod, but it was all too late. Her eyes gently closed and the side of her head came to rest against Louis's chest, she was dead.

Louis knelt down beside her. He cradled her in his arms, he said nothing and endured the pain. The anguish and the grief began to swell within him. It soon turned to rage. He again looked up towards the ceiling. A few moments earlier he had been delirious with happiness, but now, he was where he had always been. He had felt true love and had lost it, but he also realised he must still have a soul, for now it was truly tortured. He turned to the window and looked outside, It had begun to snow, for the mark of Winter had returned, the freezing weather gave testimony, the reign of Lucifer was about to begin.

About The Author

JJ Hughes was born in the Lake District in 1968. He spent his formative years in Scotland before returning to England. He now lives in Surrey. This is the first in a series of books based upon the character Louis Blue.

Printed in the United Kingdom
by Lightning Source UK Ltd.
119491UK00001B/37-42

9 781434 305701